WHISPERS

Yvonne Winston-Lawford

© Copyright 2004   Yvonne Winston-Lawford

The right of Yvonne Winston-Lawford to be identified as the author of this work has been asserted in accordance with the Copyright, Designs and Patents Act 1988.

All rights reserved. No reproduction, copy or transmission of this publication may be made without written permission. No paragraph of this publication may be reproduced, copied or transmitted save with the written permission or in accordance with the provisions of the Copyright Act 1956 (as amended). Any person who does any unauthorised act in relation to this publication may be liable to criminal prosecution and civil claims for damage.

This is a work of fiction and all characters are fictional.

First Century Ltd, 27 Greenhead Road, Huddersfield, West Yorkshire, England

E-mail: editorial@first-century.co.uk

Website: www.first-century.co.uk

Paperback ISBN 1-903930-74-X

CHAPTER 1

"You know, David, I do have to admit that I'm going to miss all of this," the young woman said as she leant against the sink unit, gazing out of the window across rooftops glistening from recent rain, idly twisting pale blonde strands of her long fine hair around her fingers.

"Don't be ridiculous, Jan," her husband who was seated at the kitchen table finishing his breakfast replied brusquely, "I certainly won't. What is there to miss?"

Jan did not reply. She continued to drink in the view she'd grown used to seeing since moving into their modest flat, a view made even more attractive by the fact that they would soon be leaving it behind. Situated in a not so fashionable part of London, their home was in actual fact just a stone's throw across the rooftops from the extravagantly renovated Docklands and the prestigious Canary Wharf, just enough distance between for their rent to have remained affordable.

She knew it all so well, for instance, where there was a narrow gap in the dense array of buildings spread out before her, she knew it would be possible to glimpse the Thames if she stood on a chair, she'd learnt that fact when she had been hanging the curtains. Today, in the early autumn light the water would appear steely grey, there would be a few boats dotted on its mirror like surface, there always were no matter what time of day.

Closer in Jan's line of vision was a splodge of brownish- green, which she knew to be the park where she took their son four year old Paul to play and, yet closer still, the huge multi-storied office block with mirror glass windows, their very composition making it impossible to see anything inside. For a fleeting moment, she reflected, , on how often she had wondered, as she had washed up, what went on behind those sheets of silvered glass.

A train, no larger than a caterpillar, came into view, making its way along the tracks in the far distance, Jan could almost tell the time by those trains. Yes she thought there was always something to see outside the window, endless activity as each day the ancient City awoke and expelled its inhabitants to go about their business.

"I'd better be off then," David drained his cup and rose from the table stretching his six foot three frame to its fullest height. He walked over to the sink and dropped the mug in the bowl of soapy water.

"Are you coming down to see us off?"

"Yes of course," Jan at last tore her gaze from the window. Her husband was taking Paul and eight month old Sarah to Jan's parents for a couple of days, in order that he could take Jan to see a house in Wales with a view to moving.

In the children's room Paul, a miniature version of his father with tawny coloured hair and big blue eyes, was curled up on the bed looking at a book, whilst the baby gurgled contentedly in her cot, legs in the air playing with her toes.

"Have you put all the toys you want to take with you in the bag?" Jan asked.

Paul nodded solemnly and slid off the bed. He pulled open the bag on the floor to reveal his favourite toys inside, to which Jan added Sarah's teddy bear and bricks before zipping closed the small holdall.

"How long are we going to stay and at Nana's and Granddad's?"

"Just for a couple of days, while I go with Daddy to see a new house we might go to live in. Then, if we like it, we could be moving very soon and you'll have a real garden to play in and a room of your own. Won't that be lovely?"

"I don't mind sharing with Sarah," the little boy said.

"I know, but you'll need a bigger room soon anyway, you are getting such a big boy now."

Paul beamed proudly at her words and looked down at his feet, in the curious way children have when trying to assess how tall they are.

He dashed off to find his father, whilst his mother sat on the bed and dressed the baby in her coat and leggings.

When they were all ready at last, the family set off down the stairs to their front door, which opened on to a busy street. The flat was situated over the top of a Tobacconist and as they stepped outside, Abe Goldstein the owner and their landlord, hurried out of the door to speak to them pulling his shapeless old grey cardigan tightly around him against the early morning chill.

Jan had become very fond of the gentle old man, and knew she would miss the cosy chats the two of them often had when David was working. Jan, once a receptionist in a busy hairdressing salon missed the camaraderie of her work colleagues since she'd left to have the children, and often found herself missing adult company when her husband was at work. Most of her friends were either still single or had not yet started families, so were working during the day. She didn't see them socially very often either, as it meant a constant search for reliable babysitters. Her parents would often travel the relatively short distance from the outskirts of the city to sit for them, but Jan and David didn't like to impose by asking them too often.

Abe had no family of his own, having lost his wife and only daughter during the war, tragic victims of the holocaust. The fact that he himself had not been with them, on the dreadful day that they had been herded together with so many other Jews and led to their death, had haunted him ever since. No matter how much time passed, he would never be able to forget that he had not even been able to say 'goodbye'. Jan knew that truth to tell, he would rather have perished with them than survived to live alone.

In a way, the attractive quietly spoken girl, her handsome intelligent husband and their two children, who occupied the flat above his shop, had become Abe's family and Jan was only too aware, that in moving they would leave yet another hole in the worn, patched up fabric of the old man's life, a realisation which saddened her greatly. He had once confided to her, that she reminded him very much of the daughter he'd lost.

"Off to view a house then?" Abe greeted them cheerfully.

Jan kissed his soft wrinkled cheek.

"Good morning Abe, yes shortly, after David has dropped the children off with my parents. You will come and visit us won't you, after we have moved, wherever we end up?" she urged.

"Yes of course you must, you will always be more than welcome," added David for he also enjoyed talking to the old man and listening to his wartime stories. Abe had taught David to play Chess and over the years, the two of them had spent hours at the game in the effort to outwit each other.

"Just you try stopping me, "the old man chuckled as he bent over the baby in Jan's arms.

"Ah," he sighed as he gently stroked her cheek and ran his gnarled fingers over her fine blonde hair, "so beautiful, one day you will break many hearts little one." Sarah chuckled at him and reached out with her chubby fingers, in an attempt to grasp his long wispy beard.

Turning then to pat Paul's head, Abe put a hand in his cardigan pocket and drew out a small bar of chocolate.

"Could I ask you to accept this Paul, you would be doing me a great favour by eating it you see, otherwise I would eat it myself and just look how fat I am becoming already?" he patted his stomach which was anything but fat.

Paul's eyes widened as he reached out and took it.

"Thank you very much," he said beaming broadly.

"You're welcome," said the old man, "now get along with you and have a safe journey, enjoy your time at your grandparents Paul." He shuffled back into the shop and with a wave closed the door."

After Jan had seen David and the children into the car, she had stood at the corner of the road watching and waving until they were out of sight. Walking back along the pavement, crowded now with people hurrying on their way to work, she decided that this would be a good time to ask Abe up to the flat, for a chat and a cup of tea.

She opened the shop door, hearing the familiar tinkle of the rusty old-fashioned bell over the door that Abe would not part with and stepped inside. There was no sign of Abe however, just his assistant Debbie, who was stacking newspapers in piles on the counter.

"Good morning Debbie, where's Abe disappeared to?" Jan asked.

The young girl, left in charge, lifted her head from counting the papers.

"Oh hello Jan. He's just popped around to the barber's to get his beard trimmed before they get too busy, he thought it was getting straggly and he was right," she laughed "I told him he'd be tucking it into his trousers before long, if he lets it get much longer."

Jan laughed. "Oh well never mind, I was just going to ask him if he'd like to pop up to the flat for a while and have a cup of tea with me and a chat that's all, nothing important."

She left the shop and once inside the flat again, found it unnaturally quiet without the children, in contrast to the sounds of London reaching her from outside. She found herself wandering around, unable to decide what to do to pass the time until David returned. She had decided not to accompany him as she had felt it would be nice to have a little time to herself, however now she had it, found it wasn't what she wanted and wished she had gone with them after all. There were a million and one jobs she could be getting on with, what with a move coming up, but somehow she didn't have the heart to apply herself to any of them.

She'd had to admit that it had been a tremendous shock when her husband had called her from his office a month previously, and elatedly told her of his sudden and unexpected promotion. Not only did it mean that he would be earning far in excess of his present salary, but also that they would need to relocate, for the position offered to him was, at the Firm's headquarters in Wales.

David worked in a chemical laboratory, beginning after leaving College, as a modest technician he had, after years of further training edged his way slowly up the ladder, to becoming a well respected employee of Carforth's, one of the major producers of drugs in the country.

She and David had often speculated on what they, as parents of young children, would like to do with their future and moving to the country one day, had been a vague consideration that neither had dwelt on for very long feeling their life was in the city. However with a move to the country shortly to become a reality, Jan found she was having some difficulty coming to terms with the fact, that she would need to make the transition from living all her life in or near a big city, to living in an isolated part of the country. Of course she would miss her family and friends, all of whom lived fairly close to them especially her parents and Abe and of course Kate, who had been her closest friend for many years. It had been Kate who had first introduced Jan to David.

All these thoughts and more were running haphazardly through her mind, as restlessly she paced the flat finally drawn again to the view from the kitchen window. The sun was gradually making its appearance from behind the clouds, causing the wet roofs to give off a haze of steam, and she wondered if it would be a nice day for their journey after all.

She knew she should be thinking about packing some of the things that they could manage to do without for a few weeks, as it was inevitable that a suitable house would be found soon. Half-heartedly, she began opening kitchen cupboards and placing things on the table ready to be wrapped. David had bought home a number of cardboard boxes for the purpose the previous evening, which were now taking up what little space there was in their small hall.

As she rummaged through the crockery cupboard, she noticed that a few of the dishes were chipped or cracked, so wrapped them in newspaper and threw them in the waste bin. She wondered idly what her new kitchen would be like; she could certainly do with one a great deal larger than this she thought looking around her. They had even had to plane some wood from the door- frame, in order to make room for a modestly sized refrigerator. The top of which was piled high with stuff that there was no room for elsewhere.

David had already viewed the house that he was taking her to see today. She knew he had been impressed, although he said little about it when he returned home, only that he thought it was more than suitable and she would be seeing it soon. He was evasive when it came to details so Jan was more than anxious to see it for herself.

In the normal way she would have accompanied David upon his first visit, but the children had both gone down with chicken pox and uneasy about leaving them with anyone else when they were ill; Jan had elected to stay behind, for they were always so fretful and clingy when unwell. It had not been an easy decision to make, for she had known that her Mother would have been only too happy to look after her grandchildren, ill or not, and naturally Jan would have liked to see the house, but her obligation as a Mother had over ridden her desire on this occasion.

David would have been happier to wait until they could have gone together, but it was not to be. Alan Jefferson, the man who was to be David's new superior, had learnt of the property being placed on the market, and told David about it immediately he had obtained the details. When he called again a few days later to enquire when David was planning to view it, he had stressed that there should be no delay, his fears being that if action were not taken quickly the house would be snapped up by some shrewd property developer, who would waste no time in demolishing the historic building and erecting a block of unsightly modern flats in its place. A less suitable addition to the outskirts of such a pretty village as Lesser Kirston, he personally had found impossible to imagine.

So David had set forth to view the property alone, meeting Alan Jefferson at a small pub just beyond the Welsh border and then proceeding to view the rambling dilapidated old property, which he had fallen in love with the moment he set eyes upon it, seeing it more as it could be, rather than what it actually was.

The decision to accept the offered promotion had been made quickly and because David had been informed that he would be expected to take up the new position with as little delay as possible, a decision on any property he saw would need to be made quickly.

He had deliberately chosen not to portray the poor state of the house to Jan when he'd returned home, feeling sure she would have grave reservations about their move. He wanted this new job more than he had ever wanted anything, not only did it carry prestigious promotion, but a salary far exceeding anything he could ever have hoped to earn at this stage of his career in chemical research. He was determined to make a success of it, and had convinced himself that once they had moved in and the house had been put into order and newly decorated; Jan would be equally as thrilled as he was.

CHAPTER 2

Kate returned her cup to its saucer and looked at her friend in disbelief.

"You are kidding?"

Jan, deliberately avoiding her gaze, stared as intently into her coffee, as if she might find the answers to her problems swirling around in the steaming liquid. Her long, fair hair fell forward, momentarily hiding her pale features and anxious expression.

"I only wish I were."

"I can't believe it."

"Neither would I if it weren't happening to me."

"You really feel as if you are being followed?"

"Yes I do."

"When?"

"Most of the time," she shifted uncomfortably in her seat, crossing and uncrossing her legs nervously. "It's difficult to explain. It's like there is someone else in the house as well. A stranger. It's a very unpleasant feeling."

Kate picked up her cup again and averting her gaze from Jan, looked thoughtfully out of the window. The weather outside was dismal, grey and gloomy with ominously heavy dark clouds filling the winter sky, the first spots of rain beginning to tap at the glass.

"What did David say?"

"I haven't told him."

"You haven't, oh Jan really, why ever not?"

"Jan sighed heavily "I don't honestly know why, it isn't that I couldn't exactly, it's just that he has so much on his mind at the moment with the new job. He has far more responsibility than he has ever had to shoulder before and he is looking awfully tired, anyway even if I were to tell him I know exactly what he'd say."

"What?"

"That it's all simply my overactive imagination."

"Could it be do you think?"

Jan shrugged, "I doubt it. I've never had feelings like this before. It began right after the housewarming party. I keep getting a compelling urge to look over my shoulder but when I give into it and look, there's nothing there and yet..." she paused, "yet it is as I have just missed seeing something," she shuddered visibly, "and that's not all, then there's the footsteps."

"Footsteps?"

"I hear them upstairs, although no one else ever does," she finished lamely, "at least if they do they never mention it, I have to admit, I don't like it here at all Kate."

Kate shook her head, thinking that if she herself had been given the opportunity to move to this large house in its delightful rural setting, she would have been positively overjoyed.

At the time the promotion had been offered, she knew that David had hesitated, but only for a moment, realising that this might be his big chance of success in his career. He could never have hoped to reach such an elevated position in so little a time, yet there it was, being handed to him on the proverbial 'plate' so as to speak, and she, along with other of their mutual friends had encouraged him to accept without further delay. David had been resentful of the fact, that his wife had not been more enthusiastic about the unexpected change in their circumstances and had discussed his disappointment with Kate on more than one occasion.

Lesser Kirston, on the outskirts of which the new house was situated, was the typical village one saw depicted on chocolate boxes and postcards. The huge former manor house, had once been exceptionally grand, but for many years its upkeep had been sadly neglected. However Kate shared David's visualization that with time and a sizeable amount of money spent on it, the house would be restored to its former elegance.

"Try to think of all the benefits," Kate urged, "it will be far healthier for the children for one thing, growing up in the countryside".

"Of course it will, I know that, but the house is so big and the woods are so close and at night-time..." she paused " it's just so unbelievably quiet all the time, added to that you have no idea just how dark it is here at night Kate," she shuddered, "in London, well it never got really dark did it? There were always lights on somewhere and noise, do you know I actually miss the noise Kate? I never thought I would miss that."

"Kate laughed "You're just an old town bird, its beautiful here, at least when it's not raining" she added, "now when did you say it began?"

"What?" Jan was finding it difficult to concentrate.

"This feeling you say you have of being followed, is it every time you go out?"

"That's just it, it doesn't happen when I'm outside, at least it hasn't so far."

Kate now became more concerned and leant forward in her chair, "What! You mean you feel you are being followed *inside* the house?"

Jan nodded miserably.

Kate startled, felt compelled to instantly look all around the room, but everything in the big, old fashioned kitchen appeared about as normal as it could possibly be, homely in fact, right down to Tinsel, the old cat slumbering peacefully at the foot of the Aga. There were no suspicious shadows lurking in corners, absolutely no impression of anything at all out of the ordinary or sinister. The kitchen was, in spite of the short time her friends had occupied the house, already showing the signs of Jan's flair for transforming a house into a comfortable home. This was reflected in the attractively arranged, dried flower arrangement on the table, the bunches of herbs hanging from the beams which crossed the ceiling, brightly coloured tea towels and Jan's cherished collection of copper saucepans, gleaming on a pine shelf.

"I suppose it could be your imagination," she pondered thoughtfully "I mean, all of this," she gestured with her arm outstretched, taking in the whole house as a whole, " lets face it, is so totally different to what you have been used to."

"Yes it is, of course it is, but I didn't feel uncomfortable, when I entered the house the first time," Jan said. "Although outside, I thought it looked the most depressing, creepy and utterly neglected building I had ever clapped eyes upon, as soon as I stepped inside the front door I felt such a warm peaceful atmosphere, I thought that we would be happy here," she shook her head, "but everything is different now... at least for me," her last words drifting away so that Kate had to strain to hear them.

* * * *

Jan's thoughts drifted back to the day in early autumn, when she had seen Challoners for the first time. Far exceeding in size the kind of property they would have looked for in the normal way, David had assured her that the huge increase in salary he would be earning in his new position, made it well within their means. The situation was of course also; much helped by the fact that the house had been sympathetically priced, in view of the major decoration and repair that was required to make it fully habitable again.

"Excited?" David asked her, as they climbed into the car ready to begin their journey to Wales.

"Of course," Jan's voice, however hard she tried not to let it show, intimated otherwise.

David started the engine and slid the small car slowly into the heavy stream of moving traffic, heading out of the city.

"You don't sound very enthusiastic, I would have thought you would be ecstatic at the prospect of moving into a large house with a garden for the children, after all you are always saying it was what you would like one day. It knocks spots off of having to walk half a mile to take Paul to the park to play, or even see a small patch of grass come to that."

"I didn't mean to sound doubtful," Jan, replied, "I suppose it's just dawned on me what a big change it is going to mean for us, leaving all our friends behind not to mention Mum and Dad." She was sure that David would empathise with her feelings, for having been orphaned at a very young age he had, since he and Jan had married, become very close to his in-laws.

He laughed, "They'll all be able to come and visit, you silly old thing, it's hardly as if we are emigrating, Lesser Kirston is only about a four hour drive from London. It will be a terrific place for your Mum and Dad to come and take holidays, and you know how much your parents enjoy their long walks in the country, whenever they get the chance."

"Yes I suppose so," Jan forced herself to swallow her misgivings and settled back in her seat, anxious not to spoil things for her husband who appeared to be as excited, as a small boy on a day trip to the seaside.

During the journey, she couldn't help but agree, when David remarked what a refreshing change it made to see acres of fields and open spaces, instead of the copious buildings, concrete and tarmac of the city in which they lived.

It was also, she had to admit, sheer delight after they had left the motorway, to be driving through narrow lanes edged with trees, resplendent in their fiery autumn colours. Fields of corn stubble stretched either side, with even a few late poppies making splodges of bright crimson, where they had missed being beheaded by the harvester.

The property they were to view was situated on the far side of Lesser Kirston, a village some fifteen miles further on from Milborough, the town in which David would take up his new position with Carforth's Chemical Laboratories.

Lesser Kirston, when they finally reached it, was just one of many small villages they had passed through en route, but prettier by far. Consisting of little more than a few mellow flint cottages with small windows, huddled together with a small Norman church, a corner shop and a lopsided, thatched roofed pub called *The Green Man*, it was all grouped haphazardly around a triangular village green, upon which stood an old stone horse trough and a rusty pump, relics of the days of horses and carts. There was a pond as well on the green with a few ducks cutting a furrow through the smooth surface of the water. The children would enjoy feeding ducks, Jan was sure.

She privately thought the village gave every appearance of having been frozen in another time, noticing also that Lesser Kirston had even retained an old-fashioned red telephone box, the like of which had long since vanished from the streets of London.

David had thought she might appreciate taking a short break in their journey to explore the village a little, but when the suggestion was made Jan declined being anxious to press on and see the house that David had told her so little about.

David had himself already looked around the village on his first trip to Wales and had been utterly enchanted, it was every bit as pretty as he had been led to believe. A wide, fast flowing river ran on the outskirts, fringed with willows and spanned by a bridge of warm yellow stone, whilst either side of the water, beyond the water cress which grew in profusion on the river banks, meadows full of wild flowers stretched as far as the eye could see, ending only at the hazy hills and mountains of Snowdonia National Park in the far distance.

Alan Jefferson, who had shown him around on that occasion, had taken him into The Green Man for lunch. The establishment had proved to be a truly traditional Inn, serving exceptionally good food and real beer, such as couldn't be found in London any more, or if it could, David certainly had never found it.

Without exception, everyone he had cause to speak to in the village that day had appeared very friendly; he had found it a refreshing change from the City, which due to its size no doubt, was always so anonymous.

Leaving the village behind them, Jan and David passed through several more miles of open countryside before reaching their destination, but at last David brought the car to a halt outside a very large pair of ramshackle, rusty wrought iron gates, one of which hung askew in a tangle of brambles, thick with blackberries. The name "Challoners" was etched on an iron plaque on one of the gates' supporting stone pillars. Jan found her breath catching in her throat and her happy anticipation wavering as she looked beyond the gates, for the drive beyond, as far as she could see was quite utterly neglected, weeds and wild flowers fighting for supremacy amongst the sharp gravel and deep potholes.

"We'll have to leave the car on the road and walk up, I'm afraid," David apologised.

"As you can see there are a stack of deep potholes which wouldn't do much for the car's suspension, the drive is in urgent need of resurfacing."

Jan unfastened her seat belt and climbed out. Closing the door behind her she peered up the drive curiously, the house itself was not yet visible, as there were far too many trees and bushes blocking it from view. She couldn't help but realise how very peaceful and quiet it was, with just the sound of birds twittering in the treetops and leaves faintly rustling in the gentle breeze. She took a deep breath, filling her lungs with the clean sweet, unpolluted air.

The two of them walked toward the house in silence each lost in their own thoughts, the drive was very long at least a quarter of a mile. Although it was autumn, it had as Jan had hoped, turned out to be a lovely day after the early showers, and she was enjoying the sun which felt deliciously warm on her back, in contrast to the unpleasant feeling of the sharpness of the gravel through the thin soles of her shoes.

Each side of the drive, tall beeches stood like sentinels, the girth of their trunks indicating their great age. Between these, shrubs and bushes long neglected, were tangled and overgrown, whilst beneath them, tendrils of curling brown bracken and clumps of long grass covered the ground. A great deal of work would be required to tidy everything it was plain to see.

There was no doubt that Jan was extremely proud of David and his achievements. She was also aware, that she should be feeling positively overjoyed at the prospect of house hunting for a new home in the country. They were fortunate in having two beautiful, healthy children, everything in fact anyone could wish for, so why she wondered was this feeling of apprehension and foreboding, wrapping itself tightly around her, causing her stomach to fill with butterflies and shorten her breath?

As if sensing her disquiet, David suddenly reached out and took her hand, squeezing it encouragingly feeling the diamonds in her engagement ring bite into his flesh with the pressure as she squeezed back.

At last rounding a bend in the long drive, she had seen 'Challoners' for the first time, with its patriarchal solemnity, austere and forbidding, heavily stamped with the mark of a house long uninhabited.

It was by anyone's standards truly a monster, immersed in deep shadows cast by the backdrop of giant oak trees, complete with arched windows and carved stone gargoyles at the corners of the eaves and clusters of unusual shaped chimney- stacks rising from the rooftop. Jan's immediate thought was that this house was the perfect bleak setting for a gothic horror movie. She found herself panicking momentarily, the house was huge, surely this was more room than she; David and the children could ever possibly want or need?

The scene laid out before her, might have appeared slightly less forbidding had the sun been shining still, but it chose that moment to disappear behind an ominously dark cloud.

A glossy blue-black raven made them both jump by suddenly letting out a loud 'caw', it then ruffled its feathers before taking off from the roof, with the lazy flapping of huge wings and swooping low over their heads.

Grey, dull, flat uninspiring grey, grey everything, was Jan's next impression of the huge sprawling house, which she thought gave every impression of having been added to over the years by afterthoughts, none of which matched the original structure, with the odd tower here and blocked up window there. Grey granite wall, laced with spidery cracks, grey, grimy windows, diamond patterned with lead, like so many dim eyes watching their approach. Even the enormous studded door was painted a depressing slate grey, peeling in places, it revealed yet more of the unimaginative grey beneath.

A myriad of weeds, had taken root in the cracked stone steps leading to the entrance, whilst ivy had sent invasive, tangled dusty tendrils scrambling down over the porch, trailing almost to the ground. Cobwebs covered many of the lower windows, several of which were cracked. A couple of giant stone urns, green with lichen, had toppled from their bases and were lying on their sides each side of the steps, spilling out weed covered earth.

Another sign that nature was slowly taking over showed in the stinging nettles that grew in profusion, having choked to death long ago any plants that might once have graced the borders fronting the house on either side of the wide steps.

An iron lamp in the shape of an old fashioned lantern, hung in the porch from a long chain, heavily rusted by years of exposure to the elements, it swung back and forwards, creaking in the slight breeze.

Jan, although she made every effort was quite unable to disguise her look of horror, at which David noticing, put an arm around her shoulders

"I know, I thought it looked pretty depressing from the outside as well the first time I came."

Jan nodded, not trusting herself to speak, her only rational thought at that moment being that this was the last place on earth she would want to move to.

"I had no idea it would be this big or indeed so isolated," Jan said looking with uneasy trepidation beyond the backdrop of tall oaks to the lawns and woodland extending as far as the eye could see, "surely we must have other choices David?" I don't mean to sound ungrateful or anything, but this place is really dreadful and its far too big anyway, let's go back and take a look around the village or even into Milborough, there must be other places for sale, anything would be better than this…" she paused shuddering " mausoleum of a place," her voice trailed off miserably.

"We can't Jan," David hung his head looking sheepish.

"What do you mean we can't, can't what?" Jan looked at him enquiringly, wondering for a moment why he looked so uncomfortable.

"We can't look anywhere else."

"What do you mean, of course we can, I know Carforths are in a hurry for you to take up the position, but they must be able to spare a few more days for us to find somewhere suitable to live."

"I mean it's too late, I've already agreed to buy this place. It's all signed for."

Jan took a step back from him her face white with shock, "David you couldn't have, please tell me you're joking, you wouldn't do something like that without telling me would you?"

Her heart racing she looked at him, his expression didn't alter and she knew that he was perfectly serious and like it or not, they were going to have to move into this dreadful place.

"It's going to be wonderful there's so much space, why when these gardens are knocked into shape we could almost open them to the public." He hoped with that remark that he could bring a smile to her face, but Jan was furious and there was no placating her

"Surely you could have found something in Milborough? As it is you are going to have to travel miles there and back to work each day, honestly David, can't you see how ridiculous this all is? This place is going to need to need a fortune spent on it, what was wrong with looking for somewhere in Milborough?"

"When I take you there for the first time you'll understand why that wouldn't have been such a great idea," David replied, "you would hate it, it's largely industrial, there are factories everywhere."

Jan bit her lip, anger slowly being replaced by bitter disappointment in her husband, that he could have done such a thing without telling her, it was quite out of character for him.

Fumbling in his pocket he found the keys, of which there were quite a number and sorted through until he found the right one to fit the front door. Fitting it into the lock he turned it, which took quite some effort but the door at last opened and with such a painful creak, it put Jan's teeth on edge. She was dreading going inside, for as the exterior of the building was so grim, she hardly dare imagine what the interior of this inhospitable house might present. She toyed with the idea of refusing and demanding David take her home right away, but she knew that if he really had gone ahead and committed them to this place, and of that she had no doubt, then she was going to have to look at it sometime, what alternative did she have?

The front door opened on to a lofty hall, the house was now revealed in all its faded glory. In the centre of the lofty hall, a wide staircase curved upward to a galleried landing. There was a strong musty smell in the air and a fine film of dust lay over the floor and stair rail. Remnants of tattered wallpaper clung to the walls, above the lower cladding of wooden panels, faded magnolias and huge blowsy roses, twined amongst glossy green leaves on the few pieces that remained intact.

The panelled doors leading off the hall to the various rooms looked to be carved from solid oak, they were very large doors, at least half again as high and wide as the doors in their flat, Jan noted.

High above their heads on the vaulted ceiling, hung a magnificent crystal chandelier laden with dust and festooned with giant cobwebs, which swayed from a slight draught. There were a few crystal drops missing here and there, but it was still splendid never the less.

At once and contrary to what she had imagined she would feel, Jan became aware of a warm comfortable atmosphere in the old house, something she hadn't expected in view of its daunting size. Her anger began to ebb away and although the building remained somewhat of a shock to her used as she was to a modern building with lower ceilings and smaller rooms, she was beginning to imagine how it could look given time and attention. Looking again at the vaulted ceiling, the hall reminded her very much of a church.

David enthusiastically led her from room to room all of which were without exception, lofty and spacious. Even without furnishings, Jan had to admit that Challoners would make a wonderful home for any one to live in. So what if it needed repairs and redecorating from top to bottom, and the grounds outside needed hours of work, she was coming to realise that it would be more than worth it.

Quite overawed she spoke at last.

"It's so, so." She was stuck for the right word.

"Grand?" David finished for her and Jan nodded solemnly.

"It's certainly that all right, but David, how on earth are we ever going to fill these enormous rooms? The few pieces of furniture we have in the flat would all fit into just one of these."

"We'll do it gradually, from antique and curio shops, it will be fun won't it? After all, we don't need to use every room straight away, we can leave some closed up until we get around to decorating and furnishing them," he looked anxiously at her seeking her approval.

Jan's answer was to cross the room and hug him tightly, relieved he picked her up and whirled her round and around in his arms.

One of the rooms on the ground floor, brightly lit from many huge windows which formed one entire end of the room, had strange dark marks around the walls, horizontal lines, evenly spaced.

"This used to be the library apparently," David, explained, "those marks you see are where the shelves were once fixed to the walls. It would be nice to replace them and start a collection of old books don't you think?"

Jan nodded, thinking that so far, it was the only room she had seen in the rambling old house that had struck her as gloomy and ancient and not quite comfortable somehow, she was happy when they moved on and closed the door upon it.

David took her hand, "I've saved the best room on this floor until last," Jan hadn't noticed until he pointed it out, that there was still one door leading off the hall which they had not yet seen behind.

Upon entering she clasped her hands delightedly, for it was truly amazing, David had not been exaggerating when he'd said it was by far the nicest room on the ground floor. Three enormous windows, with intricately carved stone surrounds, extended from floor to ceiling, completely filling the curved bay that formed one end of the room. Stained glass panels depicting Romanesque figures, crowned with flower garlands, surrounded by sprays of lilies, in the centre of each window, cast rainbow patterns on the old parquet floor, by courtesy of the sunlight, which had obligingly appeared once again.

Exquisite plaster mouldings adorned the lofty ceiling, but by far the finest feature which dominated the room was a magnificent fireplace, which was without any doubt at all a work of art, constructed of a soft, pinkish-honey coloured marble, engraved with vine leaves and cherubs, and it was every bit of ten feet high and twelve foot wide.

Jan crossed the room for a closer look and ran her finger- tips lightly over the smooth, cold surface of the marble.

"My word, this is unbelievably grand," she said, "our furniture will pale into comparison beside this fireplace."

David laughed.

"The very best Italian marble I have been told, nothing but the best for the Blake's Jan."

Either side of the fireplace were deep alcoves, one fitted with dark wooden shelves whilst the other had a beautifully carved satinwood cupboard built into it, its wood gleaming richly in the soft rays of sunlight streaming through the windows. It's beauty however, somewhat marred by a broad dull iron band trim along its front, the heavy iron again reflected in the cupboard's handles.

"This must have been an incredibly beautiful room once," Jan mused, "Can't you just imagine it David?" She wandered around, her face taking on a dreamy expression, "Heavy cream silk brocade curtains, Chinese rugs on the floor, gold velvet upholstered chairs, a gilt clock on the mantelpiece, gilt framed masterpieces on the walls, I think it would have been like that."

"Happier now then are we?" David teased, knowing full well that she was, for her face had lit up like a child's on Christmas morning.

It was indeed a fact that Jan's spirits had by now lifted considerably; she was beginning to see what David had seen in Challoners after all.

"Well at the very least," Jan joked, "if all else fails I suppose we could turn it into a rest home for retired gentlefolk."

Leaving the Drawing room they returned to the hall and hand in hand climbed the wide sweeping staircase to the upper floor to explore the rest of the house. Jan was astonished to find that there were no less that eight bedrooms, three with en-suite bathrooms.

Yet another bathroom was situated along the long winding corridor, next to one of the smaller bedrooms. Upon entering, Jan would never have believed she could have been so fascinated by bathroom fittings, as she was by those she found inside, for the pedestal basin, bathtub and the toilet of white porcelain was completely covered with a pattern of tiny blue forget-me-nots.

"Well I never," she said, "surely this must be Victorian and probably worth a small fortune."

The bathtub, which stood squarely in the centre of the room had iron claw legs and was very deep and wide, the taps of solid brass as they were on the basin also.

"I shall look forward to taking a bath in that," Jan sighed ecstatically clasping her hands together in rapture, "just look how deep it is David?"

He winked at her suggestively, "Plenty big enough for two don't you think?"

She slapped him playfully.

"Another thing, it's made of cast iron, the water will stay hot for ages, you'll be able to read an entire book, before it gets cold," he teased, knowing her penchant for reading in the bath.

Jan looked around thoughtfully, "you know what would look really good in here?" Without waiting for him to reply she went on, "an old marble topped washstand, think how attractive it would look with a china jug and bowl on the top, filled with flowers."

David couldn't help but be pleased at her greatly improved optimism, for from the look on her face when she learnt he had committed them to moving here, he had expected a row of monumental proportions to ensue.

At the end of the magnificent curved galleried landing, was a much smaller oak studded door, arch shaped and studded with heavy square iron nails.

"What's behind there?" Jan asked curiously as they approached it.

David lifted the old fashioned latch and opened the door, revealing a spiral stone staircase, with extremely narrow steps, worn to a hollow in their centre by many years of tread.

"This leads to the attics," he told her.

"Attics, you mean there's more than one?"

"Well they cover the entire roof space of the house, but are divided into two or was it three separate rooms, I can't remember, I would imagine they were servants' bedrooms, or maybe even the nursery, Victorians liked to have their children out of earshot I believe. We could make them into playrooms or further guest rooms I suppose, they have great character, beams and sloping ceiling, all that stuff, would you like to go up and take a look?"

Jan refused being anxious to go outside having caught tantalising glimpses of the garden through the mullioned landing windows they had passed.

"Apparently there are just over ten acres of ground with the house," David remarked as they were descending the stairs, "ten acres Jan" he marvelled "it seems incredible doesn't it, that where we live now, we don't even have anywhere to hang out the washing?"

They spent a long time exploring the grounds, simply because there was so much of it to see. To the rear of the house was a flint walled kitchen garden, where once vegetables for the house would have been grown. Against one of the walls was a lean to glass house, most of the panes of glass were missing or broken, but Jan could see that inside, at least one plant appeared to have survived the cold, she thought it looked as if it might be a Grape vine.

Weeds had established themselves liberally in the open beds, but Jan could imagine how they would look eventually, and found she was quite thrilled by the prospect of being able to grow their own fresh fruit and vegetables.

Leaving the walled garden through an archway, they walked around the side of the house. Over to the left, were a number of outbuildings, David explained that these were now garages but had once been used as stables and coach houses.

Crossing the drive, they reached the edge of the magnificent sweeping lawn, although in need of a good mowing, it was covered with a multitude of large Rhododendron bushes and specimen trees. Weeping birches, the kind that had peeling silvery paper- like bark on the trunks were randomly planted along with magnificent fiery copper Beeches and Blue firs, with their steely platinum blue needles. Many of them had large cones and those that had matured had fallen and littered the ground around the trunks. The grass between the trees sloped away gently; giving way to the woodlands that covered the major part of the property.

As they walked, Jan became aware of a sweet, pungent fragrance rising from the grass, bending down to investigate she found that growing amongst the grass blades were some tiny feathery little plants with white flowers, it was from these plants that the sweet fragrance was given off.

"David, how lovely, it's Camomile," she told him knowledgably.

"I'll take your word for that," he grinned.

As they reached the wood, David asked if she would like to go inside or leave it to another day.

Jan decided it would be nice to walk a short distance inside, just to get an idea of how large it might be. Beneath the trees it was very gloomy, for even though many of them had already lost their leaves, they had been planted in such close proximity to each other, little light came through the branches, also Jan realised with a start time had gone so quickly and the afternoon light was beginning to fade.

" The Agent told me that there is supposed to be a lake in here somewhere,"" David told her, "I don't know how large it is or deep, but in any event I think we should get it fenced before the children are allowed in here, just in case they find their way to it when playing.'"

Jan nodded vehemently in agreement.

"Shall we turn back now then?" David asked.

"Okay, oh wait a minute, what's that through there, it looks like a house?"

David looked in the direction she pointed, sure enough some way off he could see a glimpse of some kind of building through the trees.

"Huh how odd, well I can't imagine what can be built in the middle of a thick wood, I certainly didn't notice it on my first visit and the Estate Agent didn't mention that there were any other outbuildings, other that the old stables that is."

They wove their way through the undergrowth, trying not very successfully, to avoid snagging their legs on the many brambles, which trailed haphazardly across the ground. At last they could see the building clearly and looked at it in astonishment.

"Whatever is it David?"

The odd building stood in a clearing and was the most unlikely thing to have come across in the middle of the wood.

"I think it's what they call a Folly; many wealthy people built such structures in their grounds years ago."

"What for?"

"I don't really know, amusement I suppose, or decoration of some kind."

Well what exactly is a folly for then?"

"All I know about them is that they are usually costly ornamental buildings that serve no practical use whatsoever," he replied walking around the side for a better look, Jan followed.

"I do have a vague recollection of reading somewhere that they were built to provide employment for the unemployed, but I don't know how true that is."

The building was indeed curious, octagonal in shape; it was constructed of a mixture of warm yellow stone and in contrast grey and white flint. Further interest was created, by the addition of areas of mosaic made out of broken china in all kinds of colours and patterns. Shells also had been set in amongst the stone and circular pieces of coloured glass, which looked to have been the base of bottles.

There was just one window, which was arch shaped and above it, the building rose upward for some twenty feet ending in a conical tower. Over the door was an inscription, almost worn away; only one word could be made out 'Liberate' then no more.

"Let's go inside," Jan pushed at the wooden door hoping it wasn't locked, it wasn't but opened with some difficulty, as one hinge had broken and the door having dropped, dragged on the ground.

"Be careful Jan, it doesn't look the safest of places," David warned. Jan had however already disappeared inside, only to come out again a few seconds later looking disappointed.

"There's nothing in there, " she said, "nothing but a flight of stone steps that go up and then immediately come back down again, like an upside down letter 'V'."

"I told you," David laughed, "a true Folly serving absolutely no practical purpose whatsoever."

"Yes but all that work for nothing," Jan said looking the building up and down.

"David shrugged, "someone had more money than sense that's for sure, come on then, it will be dark soon, time to go."

As they made their way back in the direction they had come, it was beginning to become very gloomy with the fading light and Jan was feeling somewhat uncomfortable, for the wood being so very densely populated and the thick invasive undergrowth, were beginning to make her feel claustrophobic.

"I don't like it in here David," she said voicing her concerns, as they made their way back toward the lawn, "I have this feeling, that there might be something waiting behind a tree to jump out at me."

David laughed, "Oh Jan really, what a child you are sometimes?"

As it was almost dark by the time they had reached the house, they locked up and set off to return to London. Reaching it they found they were looking at the familiar city in a new light, finding it far dirtier than they had previously noticed and noisier by far, in contrast to the peace and quiet of the remote countryside in which they had spent their day, added to all that, the city was enveloped in thick damp fog.

David parked the car in their bay and locked it up. They walked back to the flat with their arms around each other, chatting excitedly about the new life, which lay ahead of them.

CHAPTER 3

Kate spoke again, instantly snapping Jan's mind back to the present.

"Honestly Jan, I really do think you must be imagining things, I am quite sure that you will feel much better when the weather improves and you are able to get out and about, after all, you haven't had a chance yet to meet anyone from the village yet have you?"

Jan shook her head; she couldn't see how meeting anyone from the village would make any difference to how she felt about Challoners, it didn't matter how many times she left the house, she always had to return.

Feeling a blanket of depression settling over her, she attempted to move the conversation on to other things. She rather wished she hadn't said anything to Kate at all now, as it hadn't helped anything.

"Have you seen any of the gang lately?" She asked referring to their circle of mutual friends.

"No, I haven't, not since your housewarming actually." Kate replied, leaning down gracefully to stroke the cat that had woken and was now draping itself around her ankles. "I've been really busy and haven't had a lot of time for socialising; no doubt I'll be seeing them this weekend though."

Upon moving in, there had been many practical matters to deal with, furniture arriving, utilities installed and of course, simply because the house had stood empty for so long, there was plenty of cleaning to attend to.

The move had taken place in January, a freezing cold day. Jan and David had planned to follow the removal van in their car, but somewhere along the way, due to an accident on the Motorway, they had become separated from it. They were relieved to find that it was waiting for them outside the house when they arrived, the driver and his mate leaning against the side of the van taking advantage of the wait for a quick smoke.

David unlocked the front door and the men began unloading the van and lugging in the furniture and boxes.

Jan took herself into the drawing room, which was empty except for their faded red velvet armchair, the first item to have been brought in. It had been dumped unceremoniously in the centre of the room and would remain there probably, until they had decided where it was best suited.

Idly running her fingers over the soft crimson velvet of the chair as she passed, Jan wandered over to the window and looked out, still finding it almost impossible to believe, that the land before her almost as far as she could see, now belonged to them.

David popped his head around the door.

"Ah there you are, I've found the kettle and cups and things, could you make the men a cup of tea Jan?"

"Of course," she replied hurrying off to familiarise herself with her new, spacious kitchen.

As she busied herself with the tea making, Jan luxuriated in the fact that there was so much room in the house; it was such a contrast to the tiny flat. Yet in spite of everything Jan felt a tiny tinge of homesickness, it really felt at the moment anyway, that they were just on holiday and would be going back to the flat again eventually.

After the removal men had finished their tea and driven off, David and Jan sat down to take a welcome rest. The day was drawing to a close and they were simply too tired to face any more unpacking, having already unpacked the few things they would be needing in the immediate future. Although exhausted, David was in a jubilant mood and produced a bottle of Champagne he had bought and hidden away for just such an occasion, and poured them both a glass. Clinking glasses he winked at his wife, looked around proudly at the room in which they sat and said "Jan we've arrived, we are going to be really happy here, I know we are."

Jan smiled and took a sip of the fizzy golden liquid, but as it spread warmly through her body, a feeling of foreboding deep in her stomach, stubbornly refused to go away.

The first few days were nothing short of exhausting, being a whirlwind of frenzied activity. As they had known it would, their furniture looked lost, forlorn and downright shabby in the imposing new surroundings. With the exception of a few new pieces, they had left buying any more until they were settled in.

David had been given a week off before he took up his new position, for which they were both grateful, with so many odd jobs to do in their new home.

They had decided which few rooms they would use for the time being and left the others closed up, until they had time to deal with and could furnish them. Bedrooms had been decided upon and Jan had chosen the en suite looking out over the drive for herself and

David, which had the added luxury of a wide stone balcony. The children's rooms were a little further along the corridor but near enough for Jan to hear them if they needed her.

There was a fitted cupboard in the main bedroom. Crossing to it, Jan looked inside to see if there were rails for hanging their clothes. Fortunately there was, one less job she would have to ask David to do. There were an array of shelves also, upon one of which was a cardboard box. Curiously Jan picked it up it was larger than a shoebox and of a very thick shiny type of cardboard, not like the kind seen around in the present day. There were metal clasps at the corners. Sitting on the bed she opened it but to her disappointment it was empty, except for one piece of card lying on the bottom. Picking it up she turned it over and found that it was a sepia photograph, the image having almost completely faded away around the edges. Taking it to the window to see more clearly, Jan could just make out a woman with a baby on her knee and a small boy kneeling beside the chair on which she sat. A man was standing behind the woman with a hand on her shoulder. Looking closer she noticed that there was someone else in the picture, someone not posed with the group but in the background, as if she was keeping out of the way and shouldn't have been in the photographers range.

None of the people were smiling, no one of that era ever smiled in photographs, or so it seemed. Their faces were still quite clear but few of the other details were. It was interesting never the less and she laid it on the dressing table to show David wondering if perhaps the people in the photograph had once lived in the house.

When she had finished unpacking the suitcases and putting their clothes away, she went to find David to ask him if he would store the empty suitcases in the attic. She couldn't find him anywhere in the house however, so went outside to look, finding him eventually at the back of the house in one of the Garages having a rummage around.

"Found anything interesting?" She asked.

He held up a handful of rusty tools, "Only these and I don't think they are of much use to anybody." He tossed them back on the bench fixed to one side of the garage wall and together they returned to the house.

They decided to get stuck into some cleaning but found it to be a task paramount to painting the Forth Bridge, for it was never ending.

"We really do need someone to help with this," David remarked for the third time that day. They had it seemed filled endless buckets of water, wiped down what felt like miles of paintwork yet still appeared to have made little real progress.

Once the phone is put in we'll no doubt have a yellow pages delivered, there are bound to be agencies listed that place domestics," he continued.

"You could always ask at the village store," suggested Jan, "perhaps they would let you put a card in the window or something"

"You know what?" said David enthusiastically, "that's the best idea yet, I'm pretty sure they have an advertisement board anyway, I think I remember seeing one, good thinking darling, I'll get the laptop out right now and type up an inviting advertisement. You never know," he grinned, "we could find ourselves a real little welsh treasure, who wouldn't mind the odd spot of babysitting as well."

"Yes, we might," grinned Jan, heaving herself up wearily from the stairs and trudging off to empty and refill the bucket once again.

They had planned a housewarming party for all the friends they would be leaving behind in the city, on the Saturday following their move, before the children came home.

The party was an enormous success, without exception, each of their friends had been impressed with David's good fortune in landing the promotion and more than just a little envious, when they saw the former Manor house, which was now his and Jan's home.

Jan had enjoyed preparing for the party, she was a good cook and it made a change from rustling up boring food like fish fingers and chicken dippers for the children. She made prawn vol au vents, filled bridge rolls, prepared huge bowls of salad and baked three different kinds of quiches, whilst David excused himself and drove to the village for a good supply of drinks.

Later that evening with the party in full swing, Jan and David found it comforting to realise that being so far from habitation, they could play their music at full volume and not be bothered by constant pleas from neighbours to turn the sound down, as had been the case in their flat in London on the few occasions they had entertained.

Things began to quieten down a little after midnight and everyone sat around the elegant marble fireplace in which a cosy log fire burned, catching up on the news.

"Where's Abe?" asked Kate, "I was sure he would have been here."

"A shadow crossed Jan's face, "Yes of course he should have been, but I had a letter from him a couple of days ago, he has gone down with bronchitis, nothing serious but enough to prevent him from coming out in this cold weather and it is a long way for him to travel."

"How would he have got here?" asked Kate, "He doesn't drive, does he?"

"No, he would have taken the coach to Milborough and David would have picked him up from the coach station," she smiled, "don't worry he's promised to get here just as soon as the weather gets a little warmer."

"Have you seen anything of the village yet?" Moya asked twirling the ornate stem of her wine glass in her slender fingers as she spoke, the firelight glinting on the magnificent opal ring she always wore.

"No, there hasn't been time yet, David has popped in once or twice to pick up a few things but I have been so busy trying to get the house straight before today, I wanted you to see it at least looking something like home," she laughed.

Jan had always thought that Moya would have been far more suited to village life than she herself, for Moya was a 'joiner'. Before any time had elapsed at all, she would have become a member of the Women's Institute and any other women's circles available, be arranging flowers in the church and baking cakes for fetes held on the village green. Not to mention knowing everyone's history within days of meeting him or her. Yes Moya would have shone in lesser Kirston; in fact Jan found she had very little difficulty indeed in imagining her with the obligatory basket looped over her arm and a Hermes scarf casually draped around the shoulders of her camel hair coat. She couldn't resist a little grin at the thought.

Tanza, their wacky art student friend, had been quietly studying Jan, "Are you still working out?" she asked, "You know you have a figure to die for and after giving birth to two children as well," she marvelled, smoothing her long flowing skirt over her ample hips self-consciously.

"I was going to the Gym at the swim centre every week, but I am quite sure there isn't one for mile around here, so I will just have to watch everything I eat I suppose and go for long walks in the countryside," she laughed.

"Well, there's certainly plenty of miles out there for you to cover, "Tanza replied, waving airily toward the window. Becoming restless, she got up from the sofa where she was sprawled and began to wander around the room, examining some of the ornaments and curios Jan and David had collected from junk shops and the like, as she went.

Hugh, a rather studious ex colleague of David's finished his mouthful of prawn vol au vent and cleared his throat noisily.

"Marcie rang me this morning," he said to no one in particular, reaching out for a slice of quiche.

"Oh did she, how is she Hugh, no one's seen her in ages?" Called Tanza from the opposite side of the room where she had picked up and was examining a rather nice Royal Worcester vase Jan had found in a street market in Stepney, just before they left.

"Well to be honest," Hugh looked apologetically at David as he replied, "She wanted to know if Jan and David has lost their minds altogether, in wanting to bury themselves in the wilds of Wales."

Jan's head shot up, "She didn't say that, did she?"

Hugh laughed "No she didn't, she simply wanted me to pass on her abject apologies for not being able to attend your housewarming, since she wasn't able to contact you herself in time, when are you going to have the phone connected anyway?"

"As soon as humanly possible I assure you," replied David, "it is all in hand, but I don't suppose anything gets carried out very quickly down here, it does seem very strange without it I have to say, its quite a distance to have to drive into the village to make a phone call."

"No mobile then?"

"I still have it of course, but not a glimmer of a signal."

Hugh nodded, "Marcie also wished you every happiness in you new home and will write in a day or so."

"I wonder if she would like to live in a place like this," Jan said, "she hates London or professes to."

"Yes," said David, "But if she had the chance to leave I don't think she actually would, she's part of London itself, the place would fall apart without Marcie."

"Like the Tower if the raven's left you mean," joked Hugh.

Marcie was something of a legend in the area of London in which she lived, although just a couple of years older than Kate and Jan, she had always appeared a lot older and was something of an eccentric. She had always dared to be different; wearing flamboyant brightly patterned clothes and always without exception spoke her mind, to the point of embarrassing those around her on more occasions than one. Beneath all of this however, she had a heart of gold and anyone who gained her friendship, held it for life. Both Kate and Jan were very fond of her and Jan was sorry she had not been able to be with them on this special occasion.

When the laughter had died, Mark, an accountant friend of David's spoke, "Are you looking forward to starting the new job?"

Mark had said little all evening, noticing the fact Jan had glanced at him once or twice wondering if anything was wrong, but Mark with his dark brooding looks, was quiet by nature and genuinely enjoyed listening to people, often waiting until late in the conversation to make his own contribution.

David hesitated a few seconds before replying and when he did his answer surprised his wife,

"I'm not sure, I feel certain that if Jeff Saunders hadn't suffered a heart attack, it would have been him instead of me who was offered the promotion. He'd been after it for a long time and to be honest he deserved it."

Jan shocked said, "What heart attack you didn't tell me David?"

"No."

"Well how is he?"

"He died."

A hush fell upon the room; the only sound being that of a log as it tumbled from the fireplace to the hearth. David crouched down and picking it up with the tongs, returned it to the flames.

"He died, as people do every day all over the world, his loss my gain I suppose." The words were spoken defensively, Jan however was embarrassed, whatever was the matter with him he sounded so uncaring? She quickly realised however, that it was simply because he felt guilty especially knowing that if the heart attack hadn't happened, the promotion would have gone to the other man, and that he David had been second best, a strange twist of fate indeed.

Aware of the shift in the atmosphere, everyone then began speaking at once, anxious to lift the mood. Jan could see that David had to make a very real effort, to push the matter out of his mind and return to his old hospitable self.

Tanza, still wandering around the room, found herself next to the carved cupboard in the alcove and began fiddling with the handle, thinking it a shame that a carpenter would have so defaced his work by the addition of the ugly iron banding and heavy handles. Brushing her fingers idly across the front of one of the doors, it swung silently open which was to Tanza, an obvious invitation to look inside.

"What do you keep in here?" she called over the noisy hubbub of conversation.

Jan looked up from her place near the fire, her normally fair complexion flushed from the heat of the flames.

"Nothing yet," she replied, " It's empty, I think we might keep all our papers in there eventually when we get them sorted out, they are still in a cardboard box somewhere at the moment, amongst all the other things that we still have to find a place for."

But Tanza wasn't listening; she was too busy reaching into the far corner of the deep cupboard, where she was certain she could see something. Seizing hold of the object, she brought it out into the light, discovering it was a metal chest, which felt quite heavy; she shook it and heard something inside rattle.

"Hey everybody, look what I've found."

Jan uncoiled her slim body from the depths of the red velvet armchair, and went over to see.

"How odd, I could have sworn that cupboard was empty," she said taking the chest from her friend.

"Do you think it was left behind by the former owners David, do you know who they were?"

He shook his head; "the guy at the Estate Agent simply told me that the house had been empty for some time, no more than that I'm afraid."

Jan took the chest from Tanza and carried it over to show him, quite large, it looked very old, constructed of heavy tin once ornately painted but the colours and pattern had long faded, remnants only remaining. The corners of the chest and the lock were heavily rusted. David made an attempt at opening it but found it to be locked.

"Hmm, no key in the cupboard I suppose?" he asked.

Tanza went back to the cupboard and felt carefully on all the shelves.

"No, afraid not, no key."

David shook the chest, by now everyone in the room was curious as to what it might hold.

"Only one thing for it then," he laughed and leaving the chest on the table, left the room to find something with which to force the lock.

"What could be inside do you think?" Tanza asked of no one in particular.

Sean, an ex college friend of David's suggested laconically that it could be someone's family jewels.

Jan laughed, "I think if it were, whoever it belonged to would have made sure they took it with them when they moved out, don't you?"

Returning with a screwdriver, David inserted it in between the lid and the base next to the lock and pushed. He found it surprisingly strong but eventually the lock gave, and the chest sprang open.

Inside was an odd assortment of objects, which David took out and laid on the coffee- table. There were some smooth, round heavy metal discs which were numbered, a thick board, folded in four, a small pack of illustrated cards and a heavy dice, which looked very much as if it might be made of solid silver.

David carefully unfolded the board, covered in a dark green velvet cloth it was ornately decorated with gilt illustrations. Around the edge, were exquisite paintings of Angels, stars, sun, moon and planets and weaving between, were numbered squares, which ran the entire circumference of the board. A superb painting of an intricately carved, open golden gate was next to the last square.

A circle in the board's centre, held more illustrations, these in sharp contrast to those on the outer edge of the board, being of fiercely evil winged beings with horns immersed in dark clouds around which vivid scarlet and gold flames leapt.

"Good gracious!" Hugh remarked excitedly, "What an interesting item, old, obviously a board game of sorts." He dabbled in antiques and was in fact quite knowledgeable on the subject.

"I wonder what you do with it, how it's played I mean?" Carly, Jan's ex flat mate, from her single days, edged closer, her long red hair reflecting the firelights glow.

"No idea," said David, "There don't appear to be any instructions with it."

Hugh had picked up the chest again and was examining it closely.

"Hey wait a moment," he said, it rather looks as if this chest may have a false bottom." With his finger he indicated, on the chest's exterior, the level at which the floor of the chest ended, it was at least two inches from the base. He pushed around the edge of the inside with his finger and suddenly there was a sharp click and the floor of the chest opened.

"Hey how did you know to do that? " A surprised David asked grinning broadly.

Hugh grinned in a satisfied sort of way at the surprised faces looking on, and felt around inside. After a few seconds prodding he pulled out something. It was a thin cylinder of rolled parchment quite yellowed with age. He opened it with extreme care, well aware that being so brittle it could crack and disintegrate before he had the chance to read what was on it. Working very slowly, he eventually managed to straighten it out.

"What we need now," he said "Is something heavy we can flatten it out with."

Jan hurried from the room returning with a huge leather bound book, an old family bible that had been passed down through the generations of her family.

"This should do the trick I think," she laughed and set the Bible carefully upon the scrap of parchment.

"Right, nothing to do but wait." said Hugh leaning back into the old worn leather chair David had insisted on bringing with him, in spite of his wife's protests at it's shabbiness.

"Coffee anyone?" Jan asked.

The answer was a unanimous 'yes' so Jan left the room to put on the percolator.

David shivered, "Does it feel cool in here to you?" Everyone agreed that it certainly wasn't as comfortably warm as it had been, so David went to fetch more logs for the fire. As he crossed the hall he was somewhat surprised to find however, that the rest of the house was very warm indeed, the temperature having dropped only it appeared, in the drawing room.

By the time he returned, Jan had the coffee ready and was handing it around to their guests. David piled up the grate with the fresh logs and flames leapt up the chimney, but the room remained cool and everyone edged a little closer to the source of the heat.

When they had all finished their coffee, Hugh lifted the bible from the parchment and found it had effectively smoothed the small piece of paper.

"Just the job," he commented with satisfaction.

The instructions, handwritten, were for the most part spidery and faded; Hugh skimmed through them before relaying the instructions to the rest of the room.

"Some of the words are so faded I can't make them out at all, but it would appear that the game is called 'Heaven and Hell', hence the Angels and demons, on the board I imagine. The object of the game, appears to be the ability to reach Heaven, by a series of 'tasks' outlined on the pack of accompanying cards, he indicated to the wrapped pack on the table, without losing one's soul and being cast into Hell." He squinted again at the parchment. "There is a section at the bottom headed *'Please Note'*, but unfortunately the lettering beneath has completely faded and I cannot even begin guess what it might say."

"I think it sounds rather too morbid to be entertaining," Kate remarked.

"Mm, it could be Victorian, they were into those sorts of things, but then again I'm not sure, certain aspects make me think it could be even older than that." Hugh peered closely at the board again, over the top of his tinted, designer framed spectacles.

"Could it be valuable do you think? I mean those illustrations alone look to be a work of art?" Tanza observed.

"Could well be," agreed Hugh, "Hey, what do you think guys, shall we set it up and give it a go?"

Jan and Kate didn't feel inclined to take part and took themselves off to the kitchen, Jan not exactly relishing the idea, of being faced with mountains of clearing up the following morning, especially as the children would be arriving home and there would be more than enough to do with getting them settled into their new rooms and surroundings.

The two women worked steadily, emptying rubbish into plastic bags, loading the dishwasher, wiping down surfaces and chatting companionably to each other. From time to time, snatches of conversation and laughter drifting from the drawing room reached their ears.

"Imagine Tanza finding that old game like that," muttered Kate straightening the pine chairs around the long refectory table.

"Yes, I can't imagine how I missed seeing it," Jan replied frowning. "I could have sworn there was nothing in that cupboard." She paused thoughtfully, and then crossed the kitchen to put some plates away in one of the wall cupboards, as she closed the door she jumped so violently, that Kate couldn't help but notice.

"Whatever's wrong?" She asked.

"Stupid isn't it, I thought I heard someone whisper behind me, it made me jump that's all."

"Come on you two, you're missing all the fun," David had entered the room and going toward his wife wrapped his arms around her.

Jan leaned back in his arms smiling up at him his boyish features belied the fact, that he was ten years older than her thirty- three years. Fine tawny hair fell across his face, almost hiding eyes that were that unbelievable blue, reminiscent of the colour of a flawless Mediterranean sky.

"Well come on tell us, what happened then?" Kate asked curiously.

"What, oh you mean that game?" David laughed, not a lot to tell really, we got it all set up, threw the dice, took the cards when prompted by throwing certain numbers, then turning over the cards to read the tasks, found they were all in Latin. Hugh read a couple out to us, but even he with his knowledge of the language, couldn't interpret the meaning. We've given up now, nice collectible item though and a jolly interesting conversation piece."

"What a shame," Jan was a little disappointed.

David grinned, "Hugh has suggested he take it to some colleagues to look at, assess its worth and so on, what do you think? Shall we let him?"

"Yes why not? It's kind of him to offer."

"He does have some notable connections in the antique world," David continued, "who knows it might just be worth a small fortune."

"Let's hope it is," said Kate, "then it could finance all the decorating you want to do to this place."

"Yes and the upkeep of the grounds," Jan laughed, "we should be so lucky, come on let's join the others," she wiped her hands, flung the tea towel on to the worktop, and followed them out of the door to return to the drawing room.

The party had wound up fairly soon after that, with everyone staying the night, dotted all around the great house in the sleeping bags they had brought with them as none of the guest rooms were furnished. They left early the following morning promising to return before too long, Hugh the last out of the front door, clutching the strange game underneath his arm. Jan had seen none of her friends since, until Kate's visit.

CHAPTER 4

Kate drained her coffee cup, "Well, I had better be getting back to the grimy old city I suppose."

"I wish I were coming with you," said Jan wistfully, the words out of her mouth before she had been able to stop them.

"Rubbish," Kate declared, "just cast your mind back for one moment, would you really want all that living in a city means again? Just think, here you have no pollution, there are lots of lovely wide open spaces, you won't have to contend with dashing for the Tube or stand in long queues in the shops, I assure you, you have the best deal, believe me."

"I'm going to miss all of those things," replied Jan stubbornly.

Kate sighed exasperatedly.

"Yes, at first you might but not for long I'm sure, give it time," she wandered over to the window. "It's stopped raining, that's good it looks as if I'll have a pleasant drive back after all."

Sure enough a watery sun was making a timid appearance in the formerly leaden sky and was lighting up the lawn, even the forbidding woods, which fringed the vast expanse of grass, no longer appeared quite so darkly menacing.

Kate stretched and took her immaculate jacket from the back of the chair draping it around her she hoisted her Prada bag on to her shoulders. "I've really enjoyed today, I'd love to stay longer but I have so much to prepare for tomorrow's presentation. " She had a responsible position in the city, which she complained about constantly, but secretly enjoyed.

"I'm sorry not to have seen David as well but guessed he would be at work of course, never mind give him my love won't you."

"You must come down and stay for a long weekend soon," Jan urged, following her friend as she made her way through to the hall.

"Thanks that would be lovely, something to look forward to."

"Bring your camera with you and I'll show you the strange old Folly we found in the wood I told you about."

Kate was a keen amateur photographer, liking nothing better than to find and photograph unusual subjects. She always used black and white film and her favourite photographs were framed and hung on the walls of the chic flat she now owned in Chelsea.

Jan stopped at the foot of the stairs.

"Paulie, come down and say goodbye," she called, "Aunt Kate's leaving now."

Paul left his playroom, where he had been engrossed in playing with his train set which was his favourite toy of the moment. He came clambering down the stairs on sturdy little legs and reaching the bottom, threw himself into Kate's outstretched arms.

"'Bye you lovely little monster," she laughed, tickling him.

Paul's reply was to deposit a big wet kiss sloppily upon her cheek.

"Is your little sister still asleep?" Kate asked, for Sarah, the baby was having a nap in her room.

"I think so, I couldn't hear her." Paul replied.

"I'll go up and look."

Jan ran upstairs and into the baby's room, and finding her just beginning to stir, scooped her up relishing the warm, damp baby powder fragrance that clung to Sarah's clothes, and carried her downstairs.

"Oh good she's awake, I'm glad I got to see her before I left." Kate took the wriggling little bundle and cuddled her close.

"See you again soon sweetheart," then she handed her carefully back to her mother. Sarah squirmed restlessly in Jan's arms.

"I expect she's hungry," Jan said, "I'll see you off first then I'll make her a bottle."

She and the children accompanied Kate outside to her car, a sleek silver Mercedes convertible, which Jan thought suited Kate's personality better than any other could. The expensive model was a measure of the success Kate had attained in her career.

Before she opened the door, Kate kissed Jan's cheek saying "Don't you go worrying about anything now, I'm sure it will all be fine, just enjoy your new role, playing lady of the Manor."

She climbed in and fastened her seat belt, then checking her appearance in the mirror, tucked her dark hair behind her ears as Jan watched enviously. Kate didn't look any where near her age, thirty-four next birthday she could have passed for ten years younger than that. Slim and graceful, in her movements, she was bewitchingly attractive with dark hair, which glinted with fiery red lights, worn carelessly in a windblown style, which was actually cleverly contrived, as Jan knew. Although she had always tried not to think about it, Jan had always felt depressingly ordinary beside her glamorous friend.

Starting the car, it roared into life as Kate revved the engine. Waving to the little group she pulled away, her words "I'll call you as soon as your phone's connected", fading on the breeze.

Jan stood and watched until the car had disappeared from sight around the bend in the long drive. Feeling at once quite lonely, she grasped Paul's hand and cuddling Sarah close, went inside and closed the door.

Settling the baby in the playpen Jan went to the kitchen to prepare her bottle. As she mixed the milk powder with the boiling water, all kinds of thoughts were running through her head. Seeing Kate again today had made her realise how much she missed her friends. It was all very well for David to say that it was only a four hour drive from London and that they could visit at any time, but it wasn't the same as being able to spend an evening with them or go out somewhere. Neither could any of them call her and suggest a quick coffee somewhere the way they had used to. No, everything was different and she didn't like it at all. She shook the bottle angrily before plunging it into a jug of cold water to cool.

In her opinion Lesser Kirston was the end of the world, so isolated a village, as to be not even marked on the map she'd once looked at, when she was still finding her bearings. She was beginning to pine painfully for the small flat, her friends and the city they had moved away from.

CHAPTER 5

The troubles began slowly.

Three days had passed since Kate's visit and so far, Jan had experienced no further unpleasant sensations, of being followed inside the house. Convinced now that it had as Kate had suggested, been nothing more than her imagination after all, she was determined to put her homesickness behind her and set to with renewed enthusiasm, to turn the old house into the home she and David envisaged.

Leaving Paul playing happily in his room and putting the baby safely in her playpen with her plastic bricks and some picture books, Jan hoped the two of them would be sufficiently occupied, to allow her to make good headway with the mammoth task ahead of her.

She had just finished filling a bucket with water and found the box of sugar soap, with which to remove any grease and dirt from the paintwork, when she heard the bell clanging at the front door. Before answering it, she glanced into the drawing room at Sarah; the little girl was quite absorbed in the scattering of colourful bricks that lay around her.

Opening the door, Jan saw standing rigidly before her, a grim looking woman of indeterminate years.

"Good morning," Jan smiled, as she spoke.

The woman replied in oddly clipped tones in the strangest voice Jan had ever heard, it wasn't loud in tone, yet it hurt her ears somehow and had an echoing quality, Jan wondered if there was something wrong with the woman's vocal chords.

"I am Abigail Grinstead."

"Oh yes,"

"Abigail Grinstead," the woman repeated again impatiently as if Jan should have known who she was. Then seeing still no signs of recognition on Jan's face, she went on "the person who replied to your advertisement."

Confused Jan said "But we didn't receive any replies."

"Hmm, I'm not surprised." The woman rapped out, "The Postmen in the village are totally useless," and skirting around Jan, she stepped smartly inside the hall.

Of all the many things that could be said of Abigail Grinstead Jan decided 'personable', was definitely not one of them.

Taller than Jan, the woman wore her jet-black hair, rolled at the bottom in a severe style, resonant of a period of time long past. The heavy black-rimmed spectacles with extremely thick lens she wore, served to do nothing to enhance her forbidding appearance, other than to magnify her cold expressionless, steel grey eyes. Her mouth was set in such a grim line that Jan had cause to wonder if the woman had ever managed to smile in her entire life.

The clothes worn by Abigail were as severe as was her appearance, dark brown thick stockings, heavy thick-soled shoes, and a belted, brown tweed coat. In her thin white hands, she carried a tightly rolled black umbrella.

She completely ignored Jan's outstretched hand and feeling rather foolish; Jan endeavoured to regain command of the situation.

"May I take your coat?"

There was, Jan mused, something not quite right about the woman and yet at the same time something vaguely familiar about her. Abigail unfastened the belt and slipped off the coat, revealing beneath a plain navy blue dress, over which she wore, a wrap around apron with pockets, of the type Jan remembered as having been worn by her Grandmother, Jan searched the recesses of her mind but was unable to place just who it was Abigail reminded her of.

"I was about to make a start in the small bedroom upstairs," Jan, said, "I'll just go and fetch the bucket and cleaning things." She made a hasty retreat to the kitchen and when she returned found that Abigail was already halfway up the stairs. Jan thought that the woman must be extremely light on her feet, as the heavy shoes she wore made no sound on the uncarpeted stairs, whereas when Jan followed, her leather soled slippers sounded more like boots on a route march. "How rude'," she thought, 'she might at least have waited until I showed her the way.'

She was about to direct Abigail to the room she had begun work in, however Abigail marched straight to it and throwing open the door disappeared inside, Jan followed meekly, feeling rather that their positions had been reversed and that she was the help whilst Abigail was most definitely in charge.

Abigail was a worker; Jan couldn't dispute the fact, for she literally steamed through the washing of the paintwork, leaving everything bright and clean. Jan had thought she might ask her a few things about the village, for example whether there was a playgroup

Paul could attend before starting school, or perhaps a Mother and baby clinic, but Abigail worked silently without inviting conversation.

Some time later, plucking up sufficient courage, Jan asked if Abigail would like to break and have a cup of coffee.

"Don't drink coffee, never have, bad for the heart." Abigail retorted, without ceasing wiping vigorously.

"Oh dear I see, well a cup of tea perhaps?" Jan ventured.

"Hmm, just as bad," the woman replied, "but if it is very weak I'll take a cup."

Almost faint with relief, Jan bolted from the room and down the stairs to the kitchen welcoming the respite, for she had found working in the same room with the woman in the uncomfortable silence, quite unnerving.

She had just finished making the tea, doubly ensuring that the liquid in Abigail's cup was sufficiently milky, when she heard Paul running down the stairs, shortly afterwards she heard him giggling and calling to her from the Drawing room.

"Mummy, Mummy quickly, come quickly and see what Sarah's done."

Setting the tray of tea down on the hall table, Jan went into the drawing room to see what he was so excited about.

Paul was sitting cross-legged on the floor by the playpen and Sarah was gurgling happily, both were looking at Sarah's bricks. Every single brick had been strategically placed, neatly one on top of another, forming a very tall, perfectly aligned tower, on the very top of which, precariously perched was a large picture book.

"You've built Sarah a tower," Jan marvelled, "You are a clever boy, but how did you manage to get that book to stay balanced like that?"

"I didn't do it Mummy. I told you, Sarah did."

"Don't be silly Paul. Sarah's only a little baby she couldn't possibly have built that."

"She did, she did, I came in and it was built." Paul was becoming rapidly upset his eyes filling. Jan looked at him then back to the tower of bricks incredulously, and just at that moment Sarah's foot kicked out, and the Tower and book came tumbling down.

* * * *

As Jan left the drawing room and walked across the hall to take the tray of tea upstairs, she realised something very odd, she couldn't hear her footsteps on the wooden floor. The floor actually creaked several seconds *after* she had walked across, almost as if something were following her. The floor should have creaked as she put each foot to the floor, it always had before, and David had explained to her that it was something to do with the way the wooden parquet panels had been laid. At once and inexplicably, she felt the presence of someone behind her, someone who was whispering her name.

'Don't look back,' she told herself, 'there's nothing there.'

She had a dreadful thought though, that if she were to look back there might be. Determined to pay no attention to the feeling, she proceeded to climb the stairs.

Upon reaching the room she and Abigail were working in, Jan began to apologise.

"Sorry, I've been so long, I was just seeing to the childr..." she broke off halfway through her last word for the room was quite empty. The bucket stood abandoned on the floor with the cloth neatly folded over the side.

"Maybe she's in the bathroom," Jan thought, putting down the tray on a chest of drawers.

She continued with the washing of the paintwork, but fifteen or more minutes passed, the tea had developed a skin on top as it had grown cold, yet still Abigail had not returned, where could she have gone?

Jan dropped the cloth in the bucket and wiped her hands on her apron sighing resignedly: perhaps she had better check the bathroom. After all, the woman may have taken ill.

As she walked along the corridor from the small bedroom where they had been working, she checked every room, although she had hardly expected to find Abigail wandering around her home uninvited.

The main bathroom door, when she reached it, was closed, had it been closed before? Jan couldn't remember and anyway she reasoned Paul could have used it since this morning. She tapped on the door calling, "Abigail, are you there, is everything alright?"

There was no reply. Jan turned the knob and finding the door unlocked went inside to check but, the room was quite empty.

She felt she had no alternative then, but to search the entire house, even venturing into the attics against her will. The attics were the one place in the house, she tried to avoid at all costs for they were very dim, the skylight in each of the rooms affording only very little daylight, being almost totally covered in a greenish mould outside. Why, in more recent years no one had ever thought to run electricity up there, she couldn't imagine, for it was large, dry and a good place to store many things, if you could only see what you were doing. She would ask David if they could afford to extend the power to the top floor sometime.

Abigail meantime, was not to be found in the attic rooms.

Jan shivered uneasily, not wanting to spend any more time up there than she had to. The dim light around her was charged with shadows lurking in the corners, and once again she had the strongest feeling that she was not alone. She couldn't wait to go back down stairs so closing the door of the last room she hurried towards the stone steps. Just before she reached them, her foot kicked against something small on the floor, sending it skittering noisily across the dusty boards. Stooping to pick it up, she found that it was a tiny metal box, opening it she saw that there were two coils of baby fine hair inside, one was blonde, the other with a reddish tinge. Feeling that it must be something hugely sentimental that someone had left behind, she slipped it into her jeans pocket to show David when he came home.

Focusing again on her help's strange disappearance, Jan's was now becoming angry, even more so when upon reaching the bottom stair, she noticed that Abigail's coat and umbrella, which upon her arrival had been placed on the hall chair, had gone. Exactly when the woman could have left Jan had no idea, for the entire time she had been in the drawing room with the children earlier, the door to the hall had remained open, and so she decided to ask Paul if he had seen anything.

"You know the lady who has been here helping me?" she asked him. "You didn't see her go out, did you?"

"I didn't see a lady Mummy, was someone here then?" Paul said curiously.

"Yes there was, she was in the little bedroom with me, washing some paintwork down, I expect you were too busy playing with your trains to notice."

"I was playing trains," Paul said " but I peeked in once to see what you were doing, but you were there all by yourself, there wasn't any lady, where is she then?"

Jan felt uneasy and there was an uncomfortable prickling at the back of her neck, what was this, was she really the only person to have seen Abigail arrive? She couldn't wait for David's return from work for being an extremely logical person; he always managed to find a simple explanation for what appeared to her, to be inexplicable occurrences.

She busied herself with preparing the children's lunch, feeling too unsettled by the experience to eat anything herself. Sarah was off her food and it took Jan ages to persuade her to finish the tiny amount. The rest of the day seemed endless; she couldn't remember how many cups of coffee she'd made and let get cold, lost in daydreams of wondering what could have caused Abigail to leave in such an odd manner.

She was rinsing the children's plates and mugs after they had eaten, when it came to her with a flash, Abigail, she was sure, resembled the woman in the faded old photograph she had found in the bedroom cupboard, not the woman with the children, but the person who had been standing looking on, in the background. She wondered if possibly Abigail could be one of her descendants for she had certainly appeared to know her way around the house, making straight for the bedroom like that without being shown where it was. Odd though that she hadn't thought to mention she was familiar with the house. Dropping the cup she was rinsing into the water, Jan raced upstairs to find the photograph to take another look.

Frustratingly, it was not where she had left it and although she hunted high and low, she couldn't find it anywhere. She supposed David must have moved it and waited impatiently for him to return so that she could ask where he'd put it.

David looked at her blankly when during their evening meal; she had asked him about the photograph.

"What photo do you mean," he asked? "I haven't seen any photo."

"But David you must have," I left it on the dressing table, I was going to show it to you but I forgot, with all that has been going on."

47

"Well I haven't moved it, what was it a photograph of?"

"It was a family, taken, well, I would think in the last century, I thought perhaps they may have once lived in this house."

"Well it has to be there somewhere," he said in his irritating 'matter of fact' voice," things don't disappear into thin air."

"Abigail did," muttered Jan under her breath.

In the next moments the missing photograph was forgotten as Sarah awoke and began screaming. She was teething and utterly miserable with her sore, inflamed gums. One or the other of her parents had to spend night after night with her pacing what seemed like miles, in an effort to pacify her. Their love for their baby tried to endurance, for as much as they both adored her, when faced with a screaming red faced infant in the middle of the night, when they were dropping with tiredness; it was difficult to feel deep affection. It was making them irritable; although both knew it was support they should extend to each other and not harsh words.

They had only once made love since moving into Challoners, which saddened Jan. of course she knew that sex was not the be all and end all of a marriage, but it certainly was an important part and she missed the warmth and closeness it brought. Jan, all her life had needed affection as other people needed oxygen to breathe, deprived of it; it had the result of making her feel physically ill.

Simply because it was worrying her, she had tried tactfully to raise the subject one evening when David had returned from work a little earlier than usual. David had admitted to her that he also was feeling a great deal of worry and guilt associated with their lack of lovemaking. His reasons for abstaining were work related he said, being always so tired, the responsibilities of his new position being largely responsible.

More than once, Jan found herself wishing David had refused the promotion and they had remained living in the little flat in London. She knew it was a sad but true fact of life that no one ever realised how much he or she appreciated anything until it had gone.

David, apart from getting up to see to Sarah occasionally, had many other nights when he would go to bed only to doze a short while before waking and getting up again. On these occasions Jan, after having struggled to get to sleep in the first place, would awaken to find the bed beside her empty and cold. She would always find her husband in the same place, sitting at his laptop at the kitchen table with a half drunk, forgotten cold cup of coffee beside him. The first time she had found him that way, she had tried to coax him back to bed but he'd snapped at her and she'd returned to bed alone, knowing in future that it was best to leave him to it.

As she was making a cup of coffee for them after dinner, Jan dropped a teaspoon on to the floor; as she bent to pick it up she felt something in her pocket, stick into her thigh. She remembered then, the little silver box she'd found and after she had handed David his cup she took the box from her pocket to show him.

"Ugh, he shuddered as he looked into it, "probably comes from dead people."

Jan grimaced, "Oh do you think so, I thought perhaps they were children's, you know their first ever hair cut?"

"Mmm could be I suppose, morbid habit keeping hair, I think so anyway, where did you find it?"

"In the attic on the floor."

"Oh well put it into the cupboard with that old game, at this rate we'll soon have a collection of old relics that someone has left behind."

The mantle clock chimed eleven, David yawned, stretching in his chair by the fire.

"I'm really sorry love," he said apologetically, "I'm just too tired to stay up any longer."

Jan uncurled herself from the sofa and went over to him, dropping a kiss on his forehead and running her fingers through his hair.

He'd looked exhausted when he'd arrived home, having worked several hours overtime. The clock had been chiming ten; as he'd sat down to eat the meal he'd been too tired to finish.

Paul had been fast sleep for several hours, having given up the struggle to stay awake long enough to see his Dad, and have him read a bedtime story to him. Sarah for once seemed to be having no trouble with her gums and was sleeping soundly.

David constantly felt guilty for having so little time to spend with his wife and children, he knew it had not been easy for them, Jan especially, leaving behind all that was familiar and moving out here, miles from anywhere. He knew also, that he had a great deal to prove in his new job and that it was necessary to put in the extra hours at the moment, but hoped that once he became familiar with the new routine and to working with a new team, things would become easier and he could cut back to working more or less a normal day once again.

Jan had decided not to mention Abigail Grinstead to David after all, at least not yet. It had happened, the woman had gone and Jan doubted she would return, so there was little point in adding to David's worries by making a big issue out of it.

"You go on up love," she said, noting with concern the deep lines of tiredness etched around his eyes. "I'll just take our cups out to the kitchen and I'll join you."

David kissed her, ruffled her hair and made his way wearily up the stairs.

Jan rinsed the cups before stacking them in the dishwasher then adding the detergent she set the machine to a basic wash programme. She was pulling down the kitchen blind, when, reflected in the darkened window, she had a brief glimpse of a shape looming behind her. She whirled around thinking it was David, but to her surprise the room was empty. She shrugged, convincing herself it had been merely a shadow or her own image, double reflected in the old glass. She mustn't let her imagination run away with her. Closing the kitchen door behind her, she returned to the drawing room to turn off the lamps and the television.

She felt strangely disorientated, the events of the day having seriously disturbed her. She moved around automatically aware that there were strange undercurrents stirring in the house. She felt she should know what was causing them but couldn't somehow grasp it.

More than ready for bed herself, she headed toward the hall finding David's jacket where he'd dropped it on the stairs as he came in. Poor David, she sympathised, knowing full well that any other time with his inordinate sense of tidiness, he would have put it away; he must have been truly exhausted. She picked the jacket up and as she did so, a small white card fell from the pocket fluttering to the floor. Stooping to retrieve it her face blanched, for it was the advert he had been supposed to put in the General stores window in the village, for help with the housework. If he had forgotten to do so, then how had Abigail Grinstead known about the position and been able to apply?

Tired and confused and feeling she was missing something important somewhere, Jan hung the jacket in the hall closet and went to bed.

* * * *

In the drawing room, only the soft ticking of the old, wooden mantel clock broke the silence of the cold winter night. The moon, full and bright, cast a cool silver path across the faded rug before the dying embers of the fire, as it penetrated a crack in the heavy velvet curtains, where they didn't quite meet in the middle. Outside, the mournful cry of an owl echoed eerily across the dark woods.

Inside the room, the Television came back on, seconds later, so did the lamps.

CHAPTER 6

David was awake and up first the next morning, fully refreshed, and ready to face whatever challenges the new day presented. Jan stirred, stretching as he got out of bed and rubbing her eyes sleepily, asked what time it was.

"It's just gone seven o'clock," he said, "there's no need for you to get up yet, the children are still quiet, stay there and I'll bring you a cup of tea."

"Thanks darling, sweet of you to offer, but I'd rather get up with you, it will be a long time before you are home this evening."

David bent over the bed and kissed her, "yes I'm afraid it will, it won't always be like this you know, just until I get used to the new routine, there is so much to learn and it is a huge responsibility, but it does get a little easier each day."

"I know," Jan lay back, closing her eyes as she listened to the sounds of David taking a shower in the adjoining bathroom. When he had finished, dressed and gone downstairs Jan got up.

She had taken her shower and was wrapping herself in a towel, when David came back upstairs and into their room.

"I've just found the television and lamps still switched on downstairs he said," surely you remembered to switch them off before you came to bed last night didn't you?"

Jan frowned, "Yes, I'm sure I did."

Perhaps there is a fault in the electrical system," David said worriedly, "We must get it checked out. I didn't think the wiring in that junction box looked too good. I'll ask around the office today, someone's bound to know a local chap we can call, the last thing we want to happen is faulty wiring to cause a fire."

Jan was alarmed, "You don't think that could happen do you?"

"I'm probably being an alarmist but at the least it could cause power cuts."

Paul came running into the room. "Daddy, Daddy, you didn't read me a story last night.

David lifted him up, "I'm sorry son, I got in very late and you were fast asleep, I'll see what I can do about getting home earlier tonight, then I can make it up to you and read you two, how would that be?"

"I think that would be okay," said Paul solemnly.

David set him down "Go and get dressed then, there's a good boy." He watched affectionately as his son ran from the room.

Breakfast was a hurried affair, David being anxious to get to work. Jan tried to urge him to slow down and eat something more than just a couple of slices of toast but he wouldn't be persuaded.

Later, waving him off from the front door, it was only after the car had disappeared around the bend in the drive, that Jan remembered she had completely forgotten to ask him about the advert.

Her heart sank at the prospect of another long day stretching before her in surroundings she hated, for at last she had admitted to herself, that she did hate the house and every single thing about it. As far as she was concerned, it was a just a prison in a God forsaken landscape, in which she was incarcerated. The feeling of being followed had returned with a vengeance and her unease was growing hourly. It was an intense awareness, a mixture of fear and apprehension that would wash over her, riveting her to the spot and compelling her to look behind her. She would do so, and then foolishly, feel almost disappointed each time her nervous gaze revealed nothing. She tried to remain rational having proved to herself that there was nothing to see. Feelings were just feelings and could be misinterpreted after all. She tried to push away the niggling thought that her subconscious was kicking in trying to tell her something, the total of all her disjointed thoughts over the last weeks in Challoners, but the feeling would not go away. 'I don't know any more' she found herself thinking anxiously,' whether it's all inside my head or inside this house.'

Each night recently she had begun hearing noises, strange sounds, which kept her awake, whilst her husband and children slept peacefully, sounds which she was far too frightened to check out. Things were if anything she noticed, worse upstairs, and each time she reached the top stair, she would pass a chillingly 'cold spot' and feel that something was there waiting for her. Differing from the presence she felt followed her, this was something new, something even more intense.

Although she longed to, she still held off from talking to David about it knowing it would only add to the worries he was carrying already.

The lovely warm atmosphere she had at first felt, had completely deserted the house although it appeared ironically, that she was the only one aware of it. Admittedly winter did little to help raise her depressed spirits, for each bitterly cold day was short, dull, and sealed in with a lead grey lid of sky. She had heard that it rained a lot in Wales and it certainly had proved to do so, relentlessly. The weather then changed and the temperature plummeted, severe frosts now took the place of rain and there were sharp icicles clinging to the guttering beneath the eaves. The sinister oaks surrounding the house, stretched their bare, black branches into the pewter coloured sky, and what little foliage there was left on the bushes fringing the lawn, had been blackened by heavy overnight frosts. The lawn itself had been turned into an expanse of sparkling white with eerie grey mist trailing its fingers over its surface from the distant mountains. Jan shivered and huddling into her fleecy jacket, hurried back inside to the children, the glistening ice covered gravel crunching beneath her feet.

* * * *

"Can we go out today Mummy?" Paul asked.

"Jan nodded, "I think so, there are a few things I need and it will be nice to have a look around the village at last. I also need to see if we can find a Playgroup for you."

Paul looked doubtful.

Jan hugged him, "It will be nice to find some children to play with won't it and make some friends?"

"I s'pose so," he said, not looking at all convinced that it was such a good idea.

"It is a long walk to the village though," Jan reminded him, "are you sure you won't mind that?"

Paul shook his head vigorously.

"Well if you get tired you can always sit on the end of Sarah's buggy."

"I'm not a baby Mum," Paul declared indignantly.

"No of course you're not," Jan hurried to assure him.

She hauled Sarah's buggy out of the hall cupboard and dressed the children warmly in thick coats and gloves and hats. David had said that eventually, Jan must have a car of her own in view of the distance to the village, but to begin with, they were not in the position to be able to afford one just yet. The huge house was proving a drain on their income, without even taking into consideration the cost of doing it up. Just to heat the place alone, especially in this weather was going to be astronomical, even given that they had decided to close up most of the rooms, leaving them unused for the time being.

Jan had laughed at David's suggestion about buying her a car, reminding him that she had yet to learn to drive anyway. Living in the city, it had not been necessary for her to learn, for the tube had been seconds from their flat and a bus route ran right past their door, even the mainline station had been within walking distance. The other problem in the city of course had been the parking, David had to buy a residents permit yearly for the meters, the cost of which had been pretty hefty, without a second, if Jan had needed one as well.

"There," she said, tucking a warm pink blanket around the baby, seated in the buggy, "That should keep you nice and cosy, now are you ready Paul?" He nodded and Jan opened the front door and began easing the buggy carefully down the steps, which were very slippery.

All at once, she began to feel very strange indeed, sweat broke out on her forehead and she was finding it hard to breathe, her legs felt as if they couldn't support her and she was shaking, whatever could be wrong? She struggled on with the buggy down the steps and had just reached the bottom, thankful that she had not fallen and was extending a hand to help Paul down, when there was a loud crashing sound not unlike that of glass shattering, coming seemingly from behind them and she turned around abruptly looking up at the house.

"What's the matter Mummy?" Paul whipped his head up in alarm.

"I'm not sure, I heard a noise I don't expect it's anything to worry about but I think we had better go and make sure don't you?"

"I didn't hear anything Mummy?"

"Didn't you?" Jan frowned; the noise had been very loud he should have heard it.

Hauling the baggy back up the steps with Paul in tow, she told him to stay with Sarah in the hall whilst she had a look around. Oddly enough the unpleasant feelings she had experienced outside disappeared immediately she was back inside the front door. She realised it must have been some kind of panic attack to which she was no stranger, having seen her Mother experience them when Jan had been a teenager. She wondered what could have brought it on, however dwelt only a few seconds on the issue, being more concerned as to what had caused the noise she had heard.

Wasting no time, she searched all the downstairs rooms finding nothing at all out of place so turned her search to the upper floor. She wondered if she should be going upstairs at all, after all, what if someone had crept from the woods at the back of the house and broken in through one of the rear windows?

As she was crossing the galleried landing, a cold draught of air hit her legs, the force of which blew one of the bedroom doors shut with a bang causing her to jump. She couldn't think where the draught had come from as all the windows and doors had been closed, with the exception of the one that had just slammed. She could feel a strong sense of a presence behind her and a voice began calling her name. She whipped her head around in response but the landing was quite empty and still. She made her way toward the bathroom as quietly as she could for to her horror she had seen a flickering light showing beneath the door. She paused briefly with her hand on the handle for she could hear sounds from inside, sounds which were becoming louder by the second. She was afraid to enter but needed to know what was happening in her home, so summoning up every ounce of courage she possessed she threw the door open wide to reveal absolute chaos.

To her astonishment, towels, bathmat, and everything free standing in the room was whirling around at high speed as if in the grip of a tornado. With a loud explosion the window imploded, sending thousands of shards of glass into the room from which she had to protect her face. Water gushed from the taps and showerhead into the bath and soon reaching the top cascaded over the side on to the floor, all was accompanied by the most unearthly screeching sound.

Horrified she stood frozen to the spot, unable to back out of the room as the door slammed loudly behind her shutting her in. She hardly had time to consider the significance of this before everything completely stopped, the noise ebbing away, the towels falling into heaps on the floor and the water stopped pouring from the taps. For a moment she stood afraid to move and then wrenching open the door, she staggered into the corridor, weak with terror.

"Hurry up Mummy," Paul's voice drifted up the stairs, "You're being a very long time."

Jan pulled herself together for the sake of the children, they must have heard it all going on, and whatever could she tell them?

"Sorry Paul, I'm coming now," her voice sounded shaky even to her own ears. Hurrying along the corridor toward the stairs, she glimpsed white flakes fluttering down outside the window it had begun to snow.

"Why were you so long Mummy?"

"I'm sorry darling, the wind had broken a window in the bathroom," she said clutching at the first feasible explanation that sprang to mind.

"Let me see," and before she could do anything to prevent it he had squeezed past her and had dashed up the stairs.

Panicking, not wanting him to see the appalling mess the bathroom was in, she raced after him calling, Paul come back here immediately," but it was too late, he had already entered the bathroom, emerging again just as she reached the top of the stairs.

"You are clever Mummy mending it so quickly."

Puzzled Jan looked past him, the room was immaculate, there wasn't even a drop of water upon the blue tiled floor, the towels were hanging neatly from the wooden rail and the window was quite intact. She blinked her eyes, opening them again, thinking this couldn't be happening, but when she opened them again, the room was still as it had always been.

As she led Paul back down stairs, her mind was in turmoil trying to come to terms with what she had seen, her head throbbed uncomfortably, surely she couldn't have imagined it all could she? It had been so vivid. Reaching the bottom of the stairs, she felt again, the brooding intensity in the house that seemed to be growing as each day passed. She must get out for a while, she needed to think and she couldn't do it inside this house.

She opened the front door and at the sight of the falling snow Paul whooped with sheer excitement.

"It's snowing, it's snowing Mummy," he cried delightedly.

Jan hauled the buggy down the steps again, feeling at once another panic attack begin to start. Fighting it with all her night she concentrated on Sarah who was reaching out with her chubby little hands chuckling, in an effort to catch the whirling white flakes that surrounded them.

They started off down the drive, Jan's legs remained shaky and her breathing irregular. She told herself that if this was a panic attack and she was pretty certain that it was, the only way to get over it was learn to control it, as she had seen her Mother do, all those years ago.

Before they had reached the gates at the end of the drive, the snow was falling so thickly that the ground was already covered.

Jan now had second thoughts about continuing to the village, for the falling snow showed no signs of letting up and as they had so far to walk, it could be very deep by the time they reached Lesser Kirsten, and then of course they still had to return by which time she and the children would be frozen. It wasn't the easiest thing in the world to push a buggy through snow either, she was beginning to discover with annoyance.

"I think we will have to go back," she told Paul, "we'll try again tomorrow, if the snow has gone."

"Can I play outside then and make a snowman?"

Jan looked at her small son, his cheeks flushed with excitement, it was the first time he had ever seen this much snow since he had been born she realised.

"Yes of course you can, but I think you should come inside and change into some old clothes first and put on your Wellington boots, if it keeps snowing like this it will soon be over the top of your trainers."

Although the panic attack disappeared completely, Jan felt the familiar blanket of depression settle around her, taking its place as they entered the great hall again. For some strange reason, today particularly, the house was full of lonely, lingering memories of another time. She'd been looking forward to visiting the village, if only to find someone adult to talk to for just a little while. Back in the flat they'd had neighbours all around them, and with the busy high street right outside the front door, there had always been someone she could chat to. Jan loved the countryside, she always had, but she had to admit she'd had no idea that she would feel so cut off when she actually lived in it.

Sarah had fallen asleep so Jan decided to leave her undisturbed in the buggy in the hall, and went to the kitchen to make a cup of tea. The house felt cool, but as she made to turn up the thermostat, she was surprised to find it was already on a high setting. Feeling one of the radiators, she found it barely warm, frowning she turned the thermostat up even higher and waited for the heat to come through, hoping that the boiler was functioning as it should be. She wondered if when David found someone to check the Electricity wiring, they could perhaps take a look at the Boiler as well. It was hardly the time of year to chance it breaking down.

Paul ran upstairs to put on his play clothes and Jan went to find his Wellingtons. She remembered she had put them in the stairwell when they had unpacked and Paul hadn't had cause to use them until today. The cupboard in the stairwell was dark and the boots were stored right at the back, where the ceiling sloped down low beneath the stairs. She located them easily but just as she bent to pick them up, a soft deep sigh sounded close to her ear. She jumped so violently she banged her head on the low ceiling and cursed with the pain, for she still had the headache from earlier. The hairs at the back of her neck prickled, as she then heard several voices whispering all around her, which filled her with icy dread, as her heart pounded painfully against her ribs. Slowly she backed out of the cupboard, looking around the hall apprehensively. As she did so the whispering rose to a crescendo threatening to overwhelm her, surely this couldn't be happening?

Paul came bounding down the stairs and the whispering ceased at once. He took the Wellingtons from her, not noticing the strange look she wore upon her face, and sitting down upon the floor, pulled them on.

Jan, walking like a sleepwalker and with the pain thudding in her temple where she had hit it, opened the front door and watched him run off down the steps and towards the smooth white expanse of snow, which covered the lawn.

"Make sure you stay where I can see you from the window," she called after him.

"Okay Mum," he called back.

Closing the door she leaned with her back against it, her eyes darting everywhere and her ears straining for the faintest remnant of the eerie sounds she had heard.

Still trembling, and struggling to regain her composure, she checked Sarah was still sleeping before taking her tea into the drawing room. Incredibly the baby had not been woken by the sounds, how could that be? Jan wondered not for the first time, if the sounds might have been in her head, yet why should they be, she had never experienced such things before? What was odd however was that neither of her children had heard them, nor had they heard the terrifying noise in the bathroom earlier and that worried her as much as anything.

Rubbing her throbbing temple, Jan drew an armchair closer to the window so she could watch Paul as he tore around the lawn kicking up snow delightedly, revelling in the absorbing world of childhood. By now, there was at least four inches of snow upon the ground, turning the garden and surrounding countryside, into a white wonderland and still the thick flakes fell. Grudgingly Jan admitted that it really looked quite beautiful, apart from the places where the sinister dark shadows were cast by the giant oaks.

Paul slipped and fell over, Jan gasped, amazed to see that her expelled breath formed a vapour cloud in front of her face. Was it really that cold in here still?

Paul had scrambled to his feet and was carrying on playing, obviously quite unhurt. Jan got up to feel the radiator again, and was relieved to find it was red hot, although it seemed to be having little effect upon the overall temperature in the room.

Before she could return to her chair by the window, Sarah let out a sharp cry. Fleeing to see what had disturbed her baby, Jan saw something that made her heart slam violently in her chest, for a large undulating dark shape was materialising around the buggy.

"Get away," she shrieked in panic, "get away from my baby," totally transfixed, she watched as the enormous dark shape rapidly shrank in upon itself and completely disappeared. The only thing remaining was a dark handprint on the wall behind the buggy that even as Jan watched, gradually faded before disappearing altogether, leaving her to wonder if it had ever really been there in the first place.

The baby sobbed with fright at the sound of her Mother's raised voice and Jan hurried to pick her up cuddling her close, comforting her until her crying ceased. She sank down on the bottom stair with the baby in her arms closing her eyes, whatever was happening to her? She was feeling, seeing and hearing things, that simply weren't there. A kind of electric silence, so heavy she could almost taste it, hung in the air and for a moment she found herself wondering if the blow she'd received to her head in the cupboard could have caused her to think she had seen something, but in her heart she knew it hadn't. Too many other strange things had begun stirring to life around her in this infernal house, long before she had banged her head.

She sat unmoving, for some time, then as the baby had fallen asleep once again, Jan lay her in the buggy and returned to the drawing room, this time taking the buggy with her, not daring to leave it out of her sight again.

Glancing out of the window to check on Paul, her anxiety and fear were renewed as she saw that there was no sign of him anywhere. The snowman he had built, a quaint little lopsided figure with a tiny head stood alone, abandoned by its creator in the vast expanse of snow covered lawn.

"Oh no," she muttered torn between anger and anxiety, for she had specifically told him to stay where she could see him. She threw open the window, letting in a gust of cold air which carried with it a flurry of snowflakes. As loudly as she could in an effort to make herself heard over the wind, she called out, "Paul, Paul where are you?" But although she listened keenly, there was no reply, she knew there was no alternative but to go out there and search for him.

It was still snowing heavily, and having been totally unnerved by the apparition she had seen or thought she had seen, she dared not leave Sarah in the house alone, the baby was going to have to go with her. Wrapping her up as well as she could, Jan made her way outside, knowing it would have made sense to have put Sarah in the baby carrier but was reluctant to waste the time it would take to find it and then fasten all the straps and things which it consisted of, knowing that the more time she took, the further Paul could be straying from the house.

Immediately she stepped outside, a panic attack began again and Jan realised with a flash of intuition that she must be suffering from agoraphobia, what other explanation was there for these absurd attacks each time she set foot outside. It was the worst attack she had yet experienced and it took every ounce of her will power to overcome it sufficiently to be able to continue and not rush back to the shelter of the house. Such was her fear for her small son's safety however that it overcame all else.

Carefully she picked her way across the lawn, afraid of falling and dropping Sarah whom she held tightly to her chest, in an effort to protect her as much as was possible from the harsh wind and driving snow, which was causing her own face to smart and eyes to water, profusely.

As she reached the strange little snowman, Jan saw the unmistakeable trail of Paul's footprints with the distinctive dinosaur print, which was on the bottom of his Wellingtons and of which he was so proud, the trail was leading toward the dark woodland at the far edge of the lawn.

"Oh no, Paul," she muttered under her breath, "Please don't have gone into the woods." She truly dreaded having to go into them again although, she couldn't have said why she feared them so much, but the fact remained that she did and ironically they made up such a large part of the land around Challoners.

As if sensing her Mother's agitation, Sarah had woken and was beginning to cry at finding herself bounced up and down as her Mother hurried across the snow, just little cries at first muffled by the warm shawl she was wrapped in.

Entering the woods, Jan began calling Paul over and over again, but the words were torn and swept away from her by the roaring wind, as soon as they left her mouth. Looking down at the wet leaves that carpeted the ground, she realised that little snow had reached the woodland floor due to the density in which the trees grew, her heart plummeted as she realised that it meant there was no more trail left to follow. Frenziedly, she whipped her head from side to side trying to guess which way her little boy might have gone. Hovering at the back of the mind was the ever-present thought that he may have found the lake, for like all small children, he was fascinated by and drawn to water and there had been no opportunity yet to have it fenced.

On and on she searched her panic intensifying as her search revealed no sign of him, low branches springing to lash her face as she forged her way through the thick undergrowth. Sarah's cries were now becoming more distressed and Jan was worried about the effect the bitter cold may be having upon her. Although the trees grew so densely, they afforded little shelter from the icy wind, which shrieked and moaned eerily. Jan's breath was tight in her chest, the cloying feeling of claustrophobia pressing painfully upon her, at times it even appeared that the trees and bushes were actually moving toward her. If she hadn't been so desperate to find Paul, she would have turned back ages ago.

Just behind a large thick holly bush Jan stopped and stared, for leading away from the bush was a neatly paved path which twisted and turned off into the undergrowth, she stepped upon it following it, glad to have some level ground to walk upon for a change, to her surprise and annoyance it came to an end abruptly, having continued for only a few hundred yards. Jan shook her head in disbelief; surely no one in their right mind would have gone to the trouble of laying a path that led nowhere, in the middle of a thick wood? Unless of course it was the same person who had built that stupid Folly, she thought angrily. She stepped off the path that had led nowhere and struck resignedly off through the undergrowth once again.

Catching her foot in a bramble, she tripped and was saved from falling only by grasping the slippery trunk of a young Hazel, conveniently near by with her free hand, the other still holding Sarah firmly, the baby shrieked at the vibration as her Mother stumbled. Shivering violently, her teeth chattering Jan stopped and listened, for above the wind, she was absolutely certain she could hear someone calling her name, not Paul but an adult male voice.

"Who is it, is someone there?" She called, but no one answered.

There was no reply to her constant calls to Paul either, even if there had been she now doubted she would have heard anything above the wind which had risen with a vengeance, the elements it appeared were turning full fury upon her.

She dared not venture too much deeper inside the woods, very aware of the danger of becoming lost herself, for the first time with David, they had stayed so little time she had been unable to get any real bearings.

At once she found herself by the Folly, would Paul have gone inside to seek shelter perhaps? She went to look, pushing the door she was met with some resistance due to the snow banked up around the step. She looked inside and called but it was obvious that Paul was not there. As she exited the door her vision momentarily blurred and she felt a wave of dizziness wash over her, thinking she might be going to faint she tightened her grip on the baby in her arms. As her vision cleared, the scenery around her had taken on a dramatic change, she was still in the wood but it was not a wood in winter for green leaves topped the trees and dappled sunlight fell to the ground through the green canopy of branches.

Two children came into view; they were holding hands and laughing, there was a boy older than the small girl with him by some three years or so, both were dressed in clothes of another era. They stopped in a clearing and began tossing a ball between them.

Mesmerised, Jan stood watching then after just a few moments, as if a door had closed blackness descended hiding the children from view and the woodland was snow covered once again.

In Jan's arms little Sarah was becoming more and more distressed, her little face scarlet and her fair hair plastered damply to her forehead as she screamed non-stop. Her little fists, had fought free of the shawl and were wildly beating at the air.

Realising that everything was against her and she was running a very real risk of becoming lost herself, reluctantly, Jan knew there was nothing for it but to turn back and seek help.

She found that finding her way back however was not easy, many wrong turns fazed her and the thick undergrowth impeded her progress. Angrily she tore herself away from one cruel bramble feeling the back of her jacket rip as she did so. At last she found herself at the top of a mossy slope she remembered climbing on her way in. Relieved to have found at least one sign that she was proceeding in the right direction, she made her way carefully down, lurching from tree to tree in an attempt to steady herself, the baby clasped tightly in one arm, still crying unceasingly. When the ground eventually evened out again, Jan was more than relieved to see Challoners in the distance through a gap in the undergrowth and trees.

Gasping for breath yet daring not to pause for even a second for fear of losing yet more precious time, Jan made her way back across the wide lawn to the house, entering by the back door, leaving only some of the intense cold outside. She found herself cursing the Telephone Company with every breath she took, knowing she was faced with the walk to Lesser Kirston to seek help, which could take her well over an hour, even if the weather conditions had been favourable. Suffused with panic and totally distraught thinking of her little boy lost in the wood in such hostile conditions, it was almost more than Jan could bear, for like all mothers in similar situations, she feared the worst.

With a grip of iron, the band of anxiety had fastened itself painfully around her chest, making it difficult for her to breathe, let alone motivate herself into rapid movement. She was physically exhausted after her race through the woods carrying Sarah, who although only eight months old was heavy to carry any distance. However, all too soon the remaining daylight would be swallowed up by the approaching night. She could afford to waste no time; she must hurry, no matter what it cost her.

Thrusting the screaming baby frantically into the buggy, she rushed toward the front door and threw it open. It took her a few seconds for her mind to register what she saw before her, for standing on the step beaming broadly was Paul.

"Hullo Mummy."

"Oh my God, my God, Paul where have you been, are you alright? I looked for you in the woods and called and called, why didn't you answer me, you naughty boy?" Although she struggled to regain her composure, her relief was such that it was causing her to babble hysterically, one question following another in rapid succession. Finally, she dropped to her knees clasping him to her, hot tears of relief coursing down her cheeks.

"You're making me all wet Mummy," complained the little boy wiping his face with his sleeve, he was quite unable to understand why she was so very upset.

"It's alright," he said "I only went for a walk with the lady."

"Lady, what lady?" shrieked Jan hysterically.

Paul started to sob afresh at her tone of voice.

"She was a nice lady Mummy, she said she liked my snowman and asked if I would like to go for a walk with her. She said she used to have a little boy like me, and then after we'd walked a long way through the wood, she brought me home again."

"Well where is she then?" Jan asked looking around wildly.

"Paul took a deep breath between sobs and looked around him, "I don't know... she was here just now, she was holding my hand when you opened the door... I s'pose she went," he ended lamely, looking down at his feet.

Jan cuddled him close. She knew she must calm down, for it was obvious that she was badly frightening him. Anyway what did anything matter now that she had him safely home again?

As he rested his head on her shoulder she glanced down at the ground, alarm bells ringing loudly in her head, for apart from Paul's distinctive footprints, nothing marred the smooth surface of the snow, what kind of woman didn't leave any footprints? 'You know very well,' a niggling voice said inside her. Pulling Paul hastily inside, Jan shut the door firmly on a scene she could bear to look at no longer. In one moment of clear thinking, she realised what was wrong, had been wrong from the very beginning, and it was as much as she could do not to seize her children and flee from the God forsaken house.

CHAPTER 7

By the time that David returned home that night, Jan had thrust any reservations she'd formerly had about worrying him with her problems, firmly aside, the events of the day having shredded her nerves to tatters. How she had managed to pull herself together sufficiently well to be able to get through the rest of that day, she had absolutely no idea.

Paul had quite recovered from the upset of earlier on and was playing happily with Sarah, when Jan went upstairs to run the water for their baths before putting them to bed. When the bath was full enough, Jan went to fetch the children's pyjamas. She had only just stepped outside the bathroom door when a terrific booming sound filled the air, on and on it went, a deep resonant boom as if there were an air lock in the plumbing. Imagining that it would have frightened the children, Jan ran downstairs to reassure them, the dreadful noise ceasing as she reached the bottom stair. She hurried in to the drawing room, but the children were still playing contentedly.

"Did you hear that funny noise just now?" she asked Paul.

"What funny noise?" Paul asked not taking his eyes off the little cars he was playing with and that Sarah was trying to wrestle away from him.

Jan was dumbfounded, she couldn't have imagined it, it had been too loud a noise and yet obviously neither of the children had heard it.

After the children were bathed and settled in to bed, in itself a mammoth task given the state of her mind by this time, she had taken herself into the drawing room and curling up in the red armchair, had stayed there unmoving. She had not switched on the television; she had no powers of concentration to watch anything. Closing her eyes she had attempted to catnap, the events of the day having tired her both physically and mentally.

As the hours crept by, her nervousness increased, although she wasn't sure why, her stomach ached with it. She knew she should try to eat something for she'd had nothing herself when she had fed the children earlier. Her head still ached, now a deep throbbing behind her tired sore eyes, she simply wanted to close her eyes and block out everything until her husband came home.

The whispering started up again, softly coming at her from all directions. She ignored it. What else could she do? The words could never be made out yet always she felt that if she could only hear what was being said, she would understand. It would be useless to leave the room, for if she did the whispering would follow, she had tried that before. She closed her eyes and relived albeit reluctantly, the frightful dash through the wood to find her little boy, then and there she resolved never to go in there again if she could avoid it.

At long last she heard David's key in the door.

"My God it's bloody freezing out there," she heard him call out. "If I didn't know different I'd think the temperature was competing with liquid nitrogen, I've got thoroughly chilled just walking the few yards from the garage."

She heard a clatter as he dropped his keys on the hall table, before walking into the drawing room to find her.

"What are you doing sitting in here in the dark?" he asked quizzically as he entered the room and switched on the lights, which momentarily dazzled her.

Without replying, giving way at last to her raw emotions, Jan collapsed into tears and getting up from the chair ran towards him, throwing herself into his arms, clinging to him with such desperation that he found himself actually afraid for her.

"What on earth...?" he was astonished, never in all the time they had known each other had he seen her so disturbed. Gently he led her back to the chair and sat her down, perching himself on the arm beside her, keeping an arm around her shoulders as she recounted every last detail of all the strange things that had been happening. Forcing herself to remain calm, she managed to stay the incoherent rush of words, which were already forming in her mind. Speaking slowly and calmly she left nothing out, finding that once she'd begun, she found it easy to tell of the feeling of being followed, Abigail Grinstead's strange disappearance, the shape she'd seen in the hall, Paul's wandering off in the snow with a strange woman who didn't leave footprints, her nightmare trek through the hated wood searching for him and the admission that she felt she had become agoraphobic. She then mentioned the booming noise she'd heard but the children hadn't ending with a vehement "I hate this place David, I believe it is haunted."

She wasn't sure what kind of reaction she'd expected him to have to such an outpouring of incredible facts, but it certainly wasn't the reaction she got and his words both shocked and frightened her.

"Don't be so utterly ridiculous Jan; I hope you aren't suggesting that we up sticks and leave now are you? Why you've hardly given it half a chance, still never mind Jan," he went on sarcastically, "never mind that we've sold the flat, and used up all our savings on the move. Yes, we'll go back shall we and see if one of our friends will let all four of us kip on the floor until we can afford something other than a tent to live in, which is about the extent of what we would be able to afford, is that what you want?" His eyes sparked with temper and she backed away from him frightened for he was clenching and unclenching his hands so hard, that his knuckles were turning white.

"I daresay I'll get used to it..." she faltered, "Its just so, so different from home and so many weird things have happened."

"Damn it," he said "I need a drink," getting up, he strode across the room to the cabinet and lifting the heavy glass decanter, their wedding gift from Kate, he splashed a large measure of whisky into a glass. There was something frighteningly disconcerting in his contemptuous treatment of her, never before had he spoken to her in such a way and she found herself watching in silent trepidation as he downed the drink in one and replaced the glass noisily on the tray.

"This is our home now Jan," he reminded her, "you would do well to remember that."

She couldn't believe that he was being so superior, as he looked into her face, his eyes locked with hers, eyes so full of contempt for her, that she was forced to turn away sick at heart with hurt and confusion. It was almost as if another person had taken the place of the man she knew so well.

For a while, an uncomfortable tension hung in the silence between them then ironically he attempted to reason with her, and of course as Jan had foreseen, he found a logical explanation for everything. He finally deduced quite calmly, that the changes in their circumstances, so soon after Sarah's birth were entirely responsible.

"After all," he reasoned, "a new baby, a new home in an isolated area where you know no one, a boisterous four year old and a husband who is having to work long hours, all that is enough to put immense strain on you, old thing," he ruffled her hair in a sudden and unexpected change of mood and display of affection. "You know perfectly well, there are no such things as ghosts."

By the time he had finished, Jan was almost convinced that perhaps all the strange occurrences had been simply figments of her imagination, almost, but not quite. There was something wrong in his logic, although she was too bewildered and upset to work out what it was.

"Very well," she conceded, "but how do you explain Abigail Grinstead turning up here for the job, if you forgot to put the card in the shop window?"

"Oh come on Jan, it doesn't take a lot of working out does it? I'd been talking about looking for help to my colleagues in the office for days, I expect one of them mentioned the fact around the village and she got to hear, you don't need to be told how fast news travels in such tight knit communities as Lesser Kirston."

"Well then why did she disappear like that?"

"She didn't '*disappear*' as you put it, she probably just realised the job wasn't for her after all, of course she should have told you before she left, but maybe she didn't like to."

Jan doubted that a woman such as Abigail Grinstead would have been worried about mincing words over anything, let alone telling Jan she hadn't wanted to continue working at Challoners and intended leaving there and then.

"Well what about the other things?" She persisted, "what about the woman Paul went off with who supposedly brought him home, the woman who left no footprints."

"Oh come on," David laughed, "It is perfectly normal and an essential part of growing up for children to create a world of make believe, don't tell me you never had an imaginary friend when you were a child? Paul's lonely that all, he needs other kids to play with, there must be a playgroup in the village, I'll make some enquiries, the sooner we get him started the better."

"None of that explains those dreadful noises I heard though."

David sighed impatiently, "Jan this is an old house, old houses make noises, and it probably was an airlock in the plumbing or something, nothing to get alarmed about."

"But the children didn't hear it, only me."

"They probably did but Paul obviously wasn't as worried about it as you were."

Jan realised the futility of arguing her case any longer, it was quite plain to see that David was going to find a reasonable answer for everything no matter what she said in her defence.

He pulled her to her feet, "Come on now, pull yourself together, go and wash your face and I'll make us a cup of tea."

Jan scrambled out of the chair, "No, I have to go and prepare your dinner."

He pushed her gently back into the chair, "No, there's no need, I ate out today."

"You did?"

"Yes, one of the problems of the telephone not being connected yet I'm afraid, the fact that I was unable to let you know, but Hugh came down. He met me at the office at lunchtime and we went to a pub and ate," he indicated a bag he'd dropped inside the door when he came in, "he bought that game back."

"Why didn't he call in to see me as well?" Jan couldn't help feeling somewhat hurt, Hugh was such a longstanding friend of them both, and it was unthinkable that he would come all this way to meet up with David, yet not call in for a few minutes to see her also.

"I don't know. He seemed in a tremendous rush to get back. I'm sure he would have called in if he'd had the time, he sent his love to you of course."

Swallowing her disappointment Jan thought ruefully, that if only Hugh had found time to have visited her today of all days, how different the whole incident of Paul's disappearance might have been.

"What did he say about the game?" She asked, with a conscious endeavour to return the conversation to normality.

"Hm, funnily enough he didn't say very much about it at all, other than he'd showed it to a few dealers but no one seemed to be very interested, not a lot of call for that type of antique I believe was the general feeling."

"Oh dear, that's a shame, I had high hopes that it might be worth something, well never mind, perhaps Paul will be able to play with it when he's older." Jan got up and taking the game from the bag, returned it to the cupboard in the alcove.

David switched on the television and sat down to watch the late news, whilst Jan ran upstairs to check on the children.

The next morning, David behaved as if nothing had happened at all as if there had been no harsh words between them the day before. Jan couldn't help a nagging feeling of having been let down, by his unexpected reaction, to all she'd had to tell him. Not only let down, she had been extremely shocked indeed, it having been behaviour she had scarcely recognised in her husband. It seemed that he hadn't even been the slightest bit prepared to give her account of the things she'd experienced any credence what so ever.

Realistically of course, she had always known that it wouldn't be financially possible for them to do anything but stick it out at Challoners, and anyway this job meant so much to David, but even so she had expected more support from him. No matter how many logical explanations he had managed to come up with, there was still no doubt in Jan's mind that Challoners was haunted. All the things she had seen and heard were not figments of her imagination. They couldn't be. They were things left over from another time, which somehow she had inadvertently become caught up in through no fault of her own.

Much later, lying in bed with her husband snoring gently beside her, Jan mulled over the events of the day, unable to clear her mind of them. There was a chill in the room, sharper than of previous nights and although she longed for sleep it persistently evaded her. A clear cold night, she could see the outline of a full bright moon through the curtains. It was very quiet apart from a few vague creaks and groans as the old house 'settled' for the night. Tossing and turning, Jan found herself watching the steady advancement of the silver shaft of moonlight penetrating the crack in the curtains, as it tracked across the ceiling as the sleepless hours ticked by.

How long it was before sleep finally overcame her, she had no idea, but hardly had she drifted off, before something woke her again. Startled she sat up, David was snoring still, one arm flung out over the side of the bed, and perhaps it had been that which had woken her.

She lay back on the pillows listening intently, the children in their rooms just a short way down the corridor were both quiet, so it had not been their stirring, which had jolted her out of the deep sleep she so badly needed.

A cold draught swept through the room, focusing briefly on her, as if some unseen person was breathing icy breath into her face. She kept very still waiting, she had a feeling this was merely the beginning of yet another strange and frightening incident; taking a deep breath she momentarily closed her eyes.

The room being so bitterly cold made her shiver, but the real cold she knew was deep inside, caused by something nameless over which, she knew she had no control. At once, there was a subtle shifting in the atmosphere and strangely, the temperature, although having dropped dramatically on her right side now appeared normal on her left, which was becoming warm. Baffled she raised her arm and passed it in front of her body, feeling the point at which it changed.

Just then, there was a spine chilling sound, which broke the silence of the night, a low, awful keening cry that tore echoing through the silent house.

A movement to the far right of the room caused her to turn her head sharply, rub her eyes and attempt to refocus them. Hardly able to believe what she was seeing, she froze in stark terror as the most unbelievable scene began to unfold before her eyes.

An elderly bearded man wearing a top hat materialised first and began walking slowly across the room, head bowed. He was wearing dark formal clothing and across his jacket was hung a white sash, he carried some kind of a staff in his hand. A number of other figures followed him, and like him they also wore the same dark clothing and white sashes. They were carrying something on their shoulders what it was exactly, Jan was as yet unable to make out.

She found herself unable to do anything but watch in disbelief, being totally unable to have uttered a sound or cried out if she had tried.

Slowly and with great dignity, the unearthly spectral procession filed past the end of the bed before her horrified gaze, in the direction of the window. As they passed Jan shrank back against the headboard.

As her eyes gradually became more adjusted to the dark, she was able to see that what was being carried on the shoulders of the figures, were two small white coffins, topped with flowers.

At the rear of the procession came a woman, also dressed in black, her narrow white features, almost but not quite concealed by the dark veiling she wore. Pausing at the foot of the bed, she lifted the veil, revealing a face so etched with grief, that Jan actually felt it for her, her throat constricting and a sob escaping her lips. The woman appeared to be young possibly even younger than Jan herself.

The woman raised a hand and pointed toward the door whispering, "Watch *your* children", the words, strangely distorted, echoed and reverberated around the room. Then lowering the veil once more, the sad looking woman continued following the pallbearers, until just in front of the window the terrifying scene faded and disappeared.

Although, every detail of the scene she'd witnessed was firmly fixed in Jan's stricken mind, she wanted to believe she had imagined it, the alternative being too awful to contemplate. Yet as the room had returned to normality, a deep uneasy silence settled around her, as if waiting to thrust some other unspeakable event upon her. After a few minutes the numbing shock ebbed away and she suddenly came to life, frenziedly shaking David awake.

As he was struggling to bring himself to full consciousness, Jan had the most terrible thought, the coffins had been those of children, the woman's words, were they an omen? Had something happened to her babies? She was out of bed in an instant and fleeing towards the door, out and down the corridor to check on them with David stumbling half asleep in her wake.

The relief she felt upon finding each of her children sleeping peacefully was beyond parallel. As she checked on Paul first, Jan felt a fierce love welling up inside her as she bent to stroke his cheek gently, before going on to check on her daughter, which was when David caught up with her, and began to open his mouth to ask what was wrong. She quickly put a finger to her lips and pushed him out of the room and gestured for him to go back along the corridor to their room. Once there, although she was loathe to do so, in case he lost his temper again, she falteringly told him what she had seen.

To her utter dismay and in complete contrast to anything she might have expected, David began to laugh. Stricken, Jan stared at him wide-eyed, unable to believe he could find anything so terrifying, remotely amusing.

"You've had a nightmare, darling that's all," he said, "there's absolutely nothing here at all, funeral party indeed, in our bedroom of all places." He put his arms around her, "You know Jan I'm becoming gravely concerned about you, I have never known you to have nightmares as long as I've known you."

"I don't," she said shortly, she was angry and wishing now that she had kept it to herself. However, why should she, surely she had a right to expect comfort and understanding from her husband, she'd always been able to in other circumstances. Once again he was rationalising and dismissing it all as being so much nonsense, not to mention being sickeningly patronising.

Sick at heart she pushed him away. "David, I cannot believe you are being so condescending, I know what I saw, it wasn't a dream and nothing you can say will convince me otherwise."

"I'll go and make you a hot drink," he said meekly.

"The last thing I want is a bloody hot drink," she shouted raising her voice as loud as she dared, in view of the sleeping children. "I just want you to believe me for once, is it really so much to ask?" Whatever makes you think I would make up such a story and as for a nightmare; don't you think I know whether I was asleep or not? I'm hardly a child after all," she was growing more furious by the second.

"Then why do you persist in acting like one, "he shouted back taking a clumsy step toward her and raising a clenched fist.

For one heart stopping moment, Jan actually believed he was going to hit her, something he had never done in all the years they had been together and she stepped back from him in alarm. His arm dropped back to his side as he quickly recovered his composure and taking her by the arm, coaxed her back to bed.

Reluctantly, Jan climbed back in pulling the covers up to her chin, bracing herself for she was afraid they were about to have the most fearful row but surprisingly, David tried to take her in his arms. Unable to respond, after the way he had behaved toward her and indignant that he thought she would forget about it so easily, she pulled sharply away and turned her back to him. Heaving an exaggerated sigh of exasperation he switched off the lamp, which evoked an immediate response from her.

"Don't."

"Don't what?"

"Don't turn out the light," she pleaded.

"My word, that nightmare really did scare you didn't it?" he said and turning the light back on again, drew the covers over his face in an attempt to get back to sleep.

"I told you it wasn't a nightmare!" she insisted.

"Whatever," he mumbled.

It took him a long while to get back to sleep, his mind in turmoil, filled with so many things, it was impossible to clear it to achieve the restful state with which sleep could be induced. He knew he loved Jan, of course he did, there was no doubt of that and the temporary cooling of his feelings towards her he was sure would pass in time. If only she would be honest though and admit to him that she was unhappy and wanted them to move back to the city. He felt he would have so much more respect for her, than her making up this preposterous load of garbage about the house being haunted. What utter rubbish, he never would have believed that Jan had it in her to come up with such an outrageous idea. Perhaps he should encourage her to become a writer; she certainly had the imagination required with which to produce a best seller he thought ironically.

The rest of the night passed uneventfully, Jan in due course slept again, through sheer exhaustion, although her dreams were beset with nightmarish images that taunted her.

CHAPTER 8

The next time Jan opened her eyes she was relieved to find that it was morning and surprised that she had managed to sleep at all after the events of the night. The kind of intense, bright white light was showing through the crack in the curtains, indicating that the world outside was still cloaked in snow.

She had not heard David get up, he came through the door already dressed, his hair wet from the shower carrying a cup of tea in his hand. He put the cup down upon the bedside table and opened the curtains, when he turned back to her again; he was wearing a concerned expression.

"I've decided not to go into work today, at least I'll go in just to sort through the mail, and then I'll come home and spend the rest of the day with you I think we need to talk"

"Oh no David you don't have to do that, I'll be alright honestly," she was now, in the cold light of day, having doubts about what she had seen last night or thought she had seen. It had been so unbelievable that maybe David had been right; perhaps after all it had been nothing more than a particularly vivid nightmare.

Before anything further could be said, Paul came wandering in looking pitifully embarrassed, his pyjama bottoms were wringing wet.

"I wet my bed," he said.

"That's okay old chap, don't worry. " David took his son's hand, "come along I'll take you to the bathroom and sort you out whilst Mummy has her tea."

"You're not cross with me are you Mummy?" Paul asked, his mouth drooping at the corners as if he were about to cry.

"Of course not darling, it was just an accident, go along with daddy, I'll be down soon with Sarah and we'll find you something nice for breakfast."

After they'd gone, Jan leant back against the pillows, sipping her tea, looking out of the window; she could just make out a branch of the oak nearest the house, coated with a thick layer of snow. If more snow had fallen in the night, it would be several inches deep by now, when would this winter be over and the sun makes its welcome appearance to chase the cold shadows into oblivion? She wondered. It was too cold, too quiet and too far from the warm comfort she felt the summer would bring. For some reason she felt that it was only during the winter that these strange things would take place or was it simply that she needed to believe that the sun would chase the spirits away?

A tiny whimper from Sarah reached her ears and draining her cup, she clambered out of bed. Wrapping herself in her warm dressing gown she hunted around on the floor for her slippers. Unable to find them, she walked barefoot to the door and gasped as she stepped on something sharp. Lifting her foot to look she saw a bright red bead of blood was oozing from her sole.

Looking around to see what she could have stepped on, she noticed a small, crinkled brown object near the end of the bed. Picking it up, she found it to be a dead rose, dried and brown, the petals at once crackled and crumbled in her fingers. On its stem was a sharp black thorn, which was without doubt what she had stepped upon. She wondered idly where it could have come from, and then, clapping her hand to her mouth, she remembered that the little coffins carried by the spectral pallbearers she had seen in the night had been topped with white roses. So it had really happened; it had not been her imagination or a nightmare after all.

Breathless with fright she sat down heavily on the bed, the rose in her fingers completely disintegrating into a small heap of brown dust, which drifted to the floor and became no longer visible.

Sounds from Sarah, now much louder than before, broke her trance and Jan continued on her way to fetch her daughter. As she strode along the corridor, she became of aware of another sound, a strange whirring noise that she couldn't identify.

Entering Sarah's room, she stopped in the doorway surprised, the baby was attempting to pull herself to her feet by the cot bars, and she was not crying she was laughing. The object of her amusement being the mobile, Jan had constructed to hang over her cot; it was made up of seven white swans. The whirring sound was coming from the mobile, for it was revolving at such speed that the swans were flying horizontally. One suddenly snapped off and was flung into a corner of the room, at which moment the mobile stopped spinning, not little by little, but coming to a complete and utter halt as if the last thing it could possibly have done, was move.

Jan, dazed bent down and picked up the broken swan, then with a cry flung it on the floor, grabbed the baby from her cot and fled from the room.

She could hardly pretend surprise, when once again David didn't turn a hair at being told of the latest incident. She had no alternative, but to accept the fact that unless her husband was to witness one of the occurrences for himself, he would uncompromisingly put it down to her 'nerves', how she wished that Sarah was old enough to speak and could authenticate what they had both seen. The few things Paul had witnessed up to now could reasonably be interpreted, as things she herself had done or brought about, he had not seen any of the truly inexplicable things and of course she was glad that he hadn't. Over and over again, she wondered why it was only she being targeted, what could she have done to have triggered off this chain of paranormal events?

Meanwhile, dismissing it all, as if it were nothing more than an irritating problem to be thought about some other time, David went off to work, leaving Jan to speculate what if anything else the day would bring. David's whole personality seemed to have changed since they had moved into Challoners, she couldn't understand why it was not obvious to him that she was living with constant anxiety and fear, he had always made her feel so safe and so wanted, how different it all was now? How different he had become, was it this house that had changed him and if it was then how?

For the first time, for a long time, Jan allowed herself to remember how it had been before they'd moved. Nostalgic images filled her mind, of how in the days before their daughter's birth, she and David had sat companionably together in the evenings, after Paul had been put to bed. Often sitting for long periods without speaking, no need for words in their ease with each other, just now and again the odd affectionate smile, such blissful times in that small crowded flat in London, Jan thought reflectively and seemingly, so long ago.

Theirs had always been a good marriage, successful, their friends called it a match made in heaven, any worries either of them had, were thought about, discussed and solutions jointly decided upon, they were to each other, everything, best friends confidants, and lovers.

There had been no hint of the unhappiness to come, it had been such a happy, safe and orderly life they had built together, the last thing that had ever entered her head, was that one day it would all come tumbling down.

* * * *

The snow outside was deep, several inches more having fallen during the night and the sky was heavy with the promise of yet more to come. Jan feeling utterly trapped, wanted more than anything to be able to walk into the village, if only to bring back some kind of normality into her life. The house was stifling her; tears of frustration filled her eyes as she looked out at the thickly falling snow, 'Even the weather's against me," she muttered ironically, not to mention the agoraphobia."

Before he'd left that morning, David had promised to get in touch with the telephone company again. He was well aware that a telephone in the house would make all the difference to them all. The post was erratic worsened by the snow of course, sometimes when letters arrived the postmark showed a date as much as two weeks previously. Since the mail was the only way for Jan to communicate with her parents and friends until such time as the telephone was connected, the arrival of the post was the high spot of her days.

Naturally, they had explored the feasibility of mobile phones but in such an out-of-the-way spot they were unable to receive a signal. This was entirely due to the fact that the villagers had protested strongly, even taking the matter to local government with a petition, when it had been proposed that a mast be erected on farmland adjacent to the village. Lesser Kirston it seemed was in no hurry to join the twenty-first century.

Paul was clamouring to be allowed to go outside and play in the snow again, but Jan was afraid to let him out of her sight. 'It isn't fair,' this house is making prisoners of us, all except David of course', she thought enviously.

Having been refused permission to play outside, her son grumpily took up his tattered bear and giving his Mother a long resentful look, left the room. A few minutes later he was back.

"There's something the matter with Tinsel Mummy, quickly come and see."

"What do you mean Paul?"

"Come and see," the little boy insisted grasping her hand and pulling her toward the drawing room. Hoisting Sarah up on her hip, as she lifted her from the high chair, Jan allowed herself to be led.

The little cat, usually so placid and quiet, was sitting on the rug hissing and spitting, its, silver grey fur standing on end and its tail fluffed up to more than twice its normal size. With claws bared, it stabbed repeatedly at the air until finally with a strangled mew, it spun around and howling fled from the room.

Paul ran after it, Jan made to follow him, but not before she had seen the black shadow appear on the wall, which slithered slowly down until reaching the floor, it disappeared.

Jan knew beyond doubt that the cat had sensed if not seen something. 'If only you could talk Tinsel,' she thought bitterly, how ironic it was that her only ally should be a cat.

CHAPTER 9

As the days went by, more and more strange things began to take place, for instance objects appeared impossibly to be moving around on their own. Jan would mislay things only to find them again later, in the strangest and most unlikely of places. Reluctant to mention it to David, knowing full well it would in all probability spark off yet another row, she kept it to herself worrying that either she was becoming absent minded or that things beyond her control were growing in intensity.

The days grew into weeks; the situation far from improving was growing gradually worse. She still heard the whispers all around her and someone constantly called her name. The cold spot at the top of the stairs continued to cause her to perspire and tremble with an incomprehensible terror, each time she ventured upstairs.

There were more problems with the electricity, with lights switching themselves on and off inexplicably, also the Television, but always when she was alone, never when anyone was in the room with her. The electricity wiring had been thoroughly checked out and found to be in perfect working order, so she couldn't lay any blame there.

February dawned with no let up in the severe weather; the whole of the country was locked in the grip of one of the worst winters it had seen for many years, snow, wind and freezing fog being regular occurrences. David was finding the fifteen-mile journey each way to Milborough a trial he could have done without, the road conditions being so poor.

Paul woke one morning complaining of a sore throat and not feeling well. Examining him, Jan found his throat was slightly inflamed and concerned that he might be running a fever for his flushed cheeks and heavy watery eyes indicated as much, she went to fetch the thermometer from their medical chest but it was missing. Was this yet another trick? Well she knew the procedure now, all she needed to do was think of the least likely place it would be and she would find it.

'Oh yes' she thought 'I am learning to be one step ahead of the evil in this house.'

Abandoning the search for the thermometer for the time being, she settled Paul on the couch and turned on the television, so he could watch whilst she continued to look for it. Sarah was still sleeping and Jan decided not to wake her, as the baby had spent yet another fretful night with her teething, it wouldn't hurt her to sleep on a little.

The thermometer finally came to light mixed up with the spoons in the cutlery drawer, relieved to have found it she was becoming more than weary of the saga of having to search high and low for things each time they went missing. Apart from the time it took, it seemed to her to be childish tricks to play.

After she had taken Paul's temperature and found it to be only very slightly raised, she went into the utility room to unload the washing machine she had filled earlier. Returning with the loaded basket, she was crossing the hall, when a loud whisper in her ear made her jump violently and the hair on the back of her neck prickled with her fear, the whispered words, too indistinct to make out what was being said. No matter how many times it happened it never ceased to frighten her and losing her grip on the loaded basket, she dropped it, spilling out the wet garments on to the floor. A light touch on her shoulder caused her to whip around feeling more unpleasant prickling along her spine, when she saw that once again there was nothing to see.

'No of course not' she thought bitterly, 'there never is,' panicking, she fled into the kitchen, closing the door and leaning with her back against it.

"What's the matter Mummy?" Paul, who had left the sofa and was sitting up at the kitchen table with his colouring book, climbed down from his chair and ran to her.

"Nothing Paul, I'm fine really," Jan struggled to regain her composure, the last thing she wanted to do, was alert him to the fact, that there was something going on the house she couldn't have begun to explain to a four year old.

"Well, if I can't go out to play, I want to go and play in my room," he said defiantly.

Jan could think of no reason to give him, as to why he couldn't, after all, what did she think she was going to do, keep them shut up here in the kitchen until David came home, and then again tomorrow and the day after that?

With misgivings, she reluctantly stepped aside and let him out of the door, but followed him and listened. She could hear nothing, but she noticed with a shock that the laundry basket sat in the middle of the hall floor, quite empty, the washing which had fallen on to the hall floor had disappeared.

Sick with unease, she watched as Paul raced up the stairs toward his room. As he reached the landing, she heard him exclaim, giggling, "Oh Mummy you are funny."

"Why?" she called, endeavouring to keep her voice even and wondering what he found so amusing.

"You've made a pattern with your washing," was his reply.

Two at a time, Jan scaled the stairs and upon reaching the top, the most extraordinary sight met her gaze, for laid neatly on the floor one by one, stretching the entire length of the landing, was every single item of her missing laundry.

* * * *

Pacing the office floor in frustration, an increasingly irate David was arguing at length with the telephone company, or at least the poor woman who had been unfortunate enough to have taken the call in the call centre.

"Would you please explain to me?" He entreated, "Just exactly what it is that is holding things up? I completed the order for this line to be installed, several weeks before we actually moved into our new home."

"Yes sir, I know, indeed you did," the apologetic women on the other end said, "but you see there are a shortage of lines into the village and special arrangements have had to be made for the laying of more underground cable, Lesser Kirston won't agree to having telegraph poles erected you see, because it spoils the look of the village."

"Damn the blessed village," David muttered under his breath.

"I beg your pardon?"

"It doesn't matter," he closed his eyes wearily, "have you any idea at all how much longer we are going to have to wait?"

"Oh yes, they are coming out to you next Friday."

"Well why couldn't you have said so in the first place?" David rapped out in exasperation, for he had been on the call for ages, or so it seemed. It certainly wasn't as if he didn't have plenty of other things he should be getting on with, he thought replacing the receiver and turning his attention to the pile of work that daily grew higher upon his desk.

In spite of having so many things to attend to, he found his attention wandering and gazed at the chilly scene outside of his office window. In spite of having impatiently dismissed all the bizarre things Jan had been telling him of late, he wouldn't be human if he were not concerned.

The house, in his opinion was a dream come true, in beautiful tranquil surroundings it represented everything anyone could want in which to bring up a family such as theirs, more in fact. Winter and its depressingly cold, grey days would soon pass, and he knew that when summer arrived the place would be transformed. He himself had rapidly settled into their new life and surroundings, having felt truly blessed when the promotion was given to him and all that went with it. Damn Jan and her overactive imagination, it was the one thing that was marring his pleasure and preventing him from being completely happy.

He knew his concentration level at work, was dropping dangerously low, as each day bought another of her 'sightings' or whatever blessed word she chose to cover such nonsense. He himself hadn't seen one single thing that was anything approaching supernatural in the lovely old house; surely if what she was saying was true it would have affected him as well?

Of late, he had begun to toy with the idea that quite possibly Jan's problem could be post- natal depression, although to be fair, she had shown no signs of it before the move. He really knew nothing at all about the condition, for example, whether it set in immediately after a baby's birth or some months later, nor was he aware of any of the symptoms that went with it. He made a mental note to call Kate sometime and ask her opinion, not now though certainly, for he had no time for any more personal calls today. Thrusting all thoughts of his family problems firmly to the back of his mind, he turned his attention to the paperwork awaiting him.

By chance however, it happened that Kate made a call to him, half way through that very afternoon. David hastily told her a little of what had been going on, not over emphasising, as he was reluctant to put too much substance to the issue.

"It's still going on then?" she surprised him by saying.

"What, you knew about it?" David couldn't believe what he was hearing.

"Well no, not all of it, it's just that when I came down, Jan did mention that she'd had this feeling that she was being followed."

"Huh, she did, did she?" he paused "she claims there's a great deal more to it now though."

"What exactly?"

"Well, for one thing she sees things that I never see, even if I am standing right next to her."

"Really? Poor Jan."

"Even before it begins to get dark, she has to have all the curtains drawn, she says she has to keep the darkness out, she has never been afraid of the dark Kate, you know that. She also hears voices, it's all really worrying I wonder sometimes if she's becoming schizophrenic," he closed his eyes, "I know how that sounds, it's a dreadful thing to say on the other hand, you don't think, well could it be something like post natal depression?" David was anxious to get his fears into the open. Without waiting for a reply he continued," she's always had wildly vivid imagination, and she does have to spend a great deal of time on her own with just the children for company, heavens knows that could be enough to let anyone's imagination run riot.

Kate listened sympathetically before replying.

"Don't you think that if the weather improved and she was able to at least get into the village and meet people it might help? I am sure the bulk of the problem is that she feels so cut off, and it is very quiet there in comparison to where you used to live. Have you taken her and the children out anywhere yet?"

David swallowed," No I have to admit I haven't, not yet, I've been so busy and just want to relax when I get home," he paused wondering for a moment if he should tell her about Jan's added problem in that she thought she had become agoraphobic. He then decided he'd told her so much already he might as well go the whole hog.

"She won't go outside the door anyway."

"Whatever do you mean?"

"She thinks she has become an agoraphobic?"

"What, Jan?" Kate was incredulous.

"Yes, apparently every time she gets outside the house she develops a panic attack."

"You must get her to see a Doctor and soon, that is quite unlike the Jan I have always known." Kate was shocked.

"Exactly, she's totally unlike the Jan I married as well." David admitted. "That's why I thought post natal depression may be to blame."

"Of course, I understand that but I'm hardly qualified to give any opinions on that having had no children myself. Have you registered with a Doctor in the village yet, perhaps you could ask at the surgery, when you make Jan's appointment."

"No, we haven't, I've been waiting for the weather to improve and the time as well really for us all to go along together and register."

"Well make sure you do it soon David, the problem sounds as if it's becoming serious."

"Tell me Kate, honestly now, did you find or feel that there was anything out of place in Challoners, when you visited?" David asked

"Not at all and I told Jan as much, the house has a lovely peaceful atmosphere, I am quite envious, I would love to live in such grand surroundings."

"She is highly imaginative you know."

"Yes I know that, but could it simply be that she is unhappy away from the city and our circle of friends?"

"I realise that must be a large part of it, I know how much she misses you all, not to mention the shops on the doorstep and everything else that goes with living in a city I suppose, but she always made such a big thing of wanting to live in the country one day. When the chance came along, I would have thought she'd be over the moon, you know Kate, I'm beginning to wonder now if I haven't made a huge mistake in accepting the promotion."

"You mustn't even begin to start thinking along those lines David, it's a wonderful opportunity for you all and personally, I think Jan should be more supportive of you in this, although maybe I shouldn't say as much being her best friend, but I have to be honest."

"I know," David sighed deeply, "never mind I'm sure we'll get around it somehow, given time."

Kate had a sudden thought," I have a few days holiday owing I could take them and come down if you feel it would help."

"Oh Kate would you, she would love to see you and after all, it isn't as if we don't have enough room to put you up is it? You have your pick of at least five guest rooms," he laughed, feeling his spirits beginning to rise.

"Okay," Kate laughed, "leave it with me, I'll see what I can arrange."

As David replaced the receiver, he felt as if a weight had been lifted from his shoulders, he found his concentration levels were much improved and by the time he logged out of his computer, only two pieces of the pending paperwork were left on his desk to attend to.

* * * *

Wearily Jan picked up the laundry from the landing floor, apart from anything else she thought wryly, it now had to be washed again. She'd thought at first she had managed to convince Paul that she had dropped it, but knew she'd underestimated her four year olds intelligence when he'd given her a withering look.

He vanished into his room to play but came out several seconds later looking very unhappy indeed.

"Mummy, my engine's gone."

Jan opened her eyes and shook herself mentally, having drifted somewhere in her mind for a few seconds. She'd had the strangest feeling for a moment that if she stood there quietly for long enough, Challoners' mysteries would reveal themselves to her. With difficulty, she wrenched herself back from her daydreaming.

"What do you mean Paul? I saw it on the track in your room earlier."

"I know it was, but it isn't there now," the little boy persisted anxiously.

Jan heaved a deep sigh, feeling irritated and on edge, she knew she shouldn't take her worry and anxiety out on her son, after all none of this was his fault she thought guiltily as she watched him return to his room, confident in the knowledge that his Mother would soon put things right in his little world. Except that this was one time that she couldn't, for as Paul had said, the train was not on the track and furthermore a search revealed, that it was not anywhere in his room either

Sitting on the floor with a small mountain of toys surrounding her, which had been tipped out of the toy-box in the search, Jan admitted being utterly perplexed.

"You must have put it somewhere else Paul and forgotten you moved it," she insisted.

Tears welled up in Paul's eyes; he rubbed them away with the back of his little fist.

"I didn't."

Together they searched downstairs, everywhere in fact, until Jan was forced to abandon the search to feed Sarah, who had woken and was crying fretfully.

Paul went on looking for the missing toy whilst Jan attended to the baby, but by the time she had finished, it had still not turned up and Paul was becoming more and more distressed and refusing adamantly to be comforted. Jan couldn't blame him, for from the moment the train had been put into his hands it had been his favourite, he idolised it, spending hour after hour playing with it.

They had indeed looked everywhere searching each room systematically, under cushions, behind the curtains, they had even looked in places it couldn't possibly have been, for as Kate knew only too well, if it had been moved supernaturally as she was sure it had, it would not be found in any likely place. However, they did not find it; it was as if the train had vanished off the face of the earth. Unlike all the other things that went missing, but turned up eventually, this one, it appeared had gone for good, defying all previous predictability.

It had still not been found when it was time for Paul to go to bed. Jan tucked him in, her heart contracting as he turned up his tearstained face for her goodnight kiss.

"Don't worry darling," she said in an attempt to appease, "Daddy and I will buy you another if we don't find it again."

"I don't want another one, it won't be the same," Paul muttered, burying his face in his pillow.

Jan switched on his little nightlight and leaving the door ajar, returned downstairs, gritting her teeth as she passed through the 'cold spot'. She went into the kitchen to put the kettle on and as she filled it, noticed that the blooms on the African violets she had brought with her from the flat and arrayed on her new windowsill, were drooping. She lifted the leaves of each plant carefully watering beneath them, knowing that even a single drop of water on just one leaf, would cause the plant to decay. She had just watered the last of them, when she heard a series of tinkling notes.

Lifting her head to listen, she recognised it as being her Music Box, a treasured possession left to her by her Grandmother. When the lid of the box was opened, the tune that played was Brahms Lullaby. She had given the box a new home on the marble mantelpiece when they had moved and Paul had strict instructions never to touch it, as it was old and frail. What, she wondered irritably could have induced him to get out of bed, come downstairs and do so now?

She hurried to the drawing room, ready to reprimand him but to her surprise there was no sign of him and the box although playing still, had the lid firmly closed.

That evening Jan found herself even more unsettled and restless than ever; no matter how she tried she couldn't apply her thoughts or attention to anything. She didn't want to read, there was nothing to interest her on the television and she found herself utterly bored. Paul quite recovered from his sore throat and slight fever of earlier was sleeping peacefully, Sarah also for once was sleeping undisturbed.

The hours passed depressingly slowly for Jan, long hours in which she sat drinking endless cups of coffee and listening to the wind howling outside, whipping up the snow.

When the knocking began, softly at first, she thought it was coming from the back door but even as she tentatively made her way toward it, the knocking came again, louder this time from behind her in the direction of the hall, accompanied by the hated whispering.

In a panic, she ran around the house checking that all the doors and windows were locked then reproached herself for being so foolish. After all it wasn't as she were locking anything out, but rather that she was locking something in, for she was convinced that there was nothing outside that could match the evil that permeated the walls of Challoners.

Ignoring the knocking that began again and which continued to come from a different direction each time, Jan crossed to the window to pull down the blind hoping that David would soon be home.

The scene outside was crystal clear lit by a brilliantly full moon, which showed in stark relief the dark shadows of the oaks on the glistening blue- white snow and in spite of the relatively clear sky, it had begun snowing again. Shivering at the unearthly chilly scene Jan quickly pulled the blind down blotting it out.

On reflection, Jan felt she had many moments when she did begin to actually wonder if she could be losing her mind. After all it wasn't as if anyone else in the house ever saw or felt anything. Of course she was only too pleased that Paul hadn't, but if only David could, just once, she would feel so much better. She needed him to believe her, to put their marriage back on the same comfortable footing it had used to be.

Time and time again, she would hear someone calling her, someone whose voice was vaguely familiar, but although she racked her brains, the memory of just whose voice it resembled, eluded her. The weather did nothing to help raise her depressed state either, for heavy snow showers were a daily event, winter showed no sign of abating.

"Damn this infernal weather," she swore under her breath, then nervously giggled as she had a sudden mental picture of it snowing and snowing non stop, the snow piling higher in drifts against the walls, until it completely swallowed the house and all inside.

CHAPTER 9

David was elated to discover Kate waiting for him in the office foyer, a few days later when he left off work. He hugged her enthusiastically and escorted her to her car in the visitor's car, where she waited for him to fetch his own so she could follow him back to Challoners.

A surge of unexpected emotion had threatened to overwhelm him as he hugged her; startled he had withdrawn his arms quickly, as though her touch had burnt, if Kate had been surprised she hadn't shown it. She had felt good in his arms, dressed flawlessly as always and wafting the familiar expensive perfume she always wore. Jan had let herself go lately and he found himself comparing the two women guiltily, even knowing it wasn't fair, after all, Kate had no small children to run around after, and all the time in the world to attend to her immaculate clothes and appearance.

There had been a time, before he'd met and fallen in love with Jan, that it could have been Kate with whom he had chosen to spend the rest of his life for he had met her first, but somehow, work and other commitments had always intervened, each time he had tried getting close to her. Then she had begun dating a colleague of his, which had placed her firmly out of bounds. Now, suddenly for no apparent reason, the strong attraction she had once held for him, came flooding back and he had to make a conscious effort to push it from his mind.

All these thoughts and more were coursing through his mind as he made his way towards his car. Reaching it he then had to spend a good few minutes scraping the ice and snow from the windscreen. Realising he had left his can of de-icer behind, he used one of plastic store cards that he found to be extremely effective.

At last the screen was clear and he was able to drive out to the entrance to meet up with Kate, who proceeded to follow him after giving him a little wave.

Soon the smooth, wide main road they travelled on and which the local council, had cleared of snow, gave way to snowbound narrow lanes as the two cars left the town making their way into the countryside towards Lesser Kirston.

As they passed the snow capped village sign post, Kate found herself idly wondering if there was a 'Greater Kirston' somewhere and made a mental note to ask Jan and David some time.

Due to the fresh fall of snow, which had been considerable, the lane as they approached Challoners, was even more hazardous than David had found it that morning. Twice his car skidded on concealed black ice and veered into the verge; luckily Kate was keeping sufficient distance between them and avoided sliding into him.

He could hardly wait to get home to see the expression on Jan's face, when she saw whom he had with him. Kate and she always appeared to get on so well together in spite of being vastly different in personality, it was going to be quite something to be able to bring a smile to her face once again he thought. Kate had said she could only stay four or five days at the most, but even for that David was grateful.

Turning into the gates of Challoners, the tyres crunching on the frozen snow, he proceeded slowly along the drive, for the snow was even deeper than in the lane. He brought the car to a halt, in front of the garages to the rear of the house deciding he would let Kate inside in the warm first, then after dinner would put both cars away, giving the women some time on their own. He hoped that perhaps Jan would confide in Kate and that perhaps Kate could allay some of her fears.

Together they walked to the front door, David supporting Kate as their feet sank into the deep snow. Kate was having the utmost difficulty in walking, wearing as she always did three-inch high stiletto heeled shoes.

As they approached the front door David suddenly noticed something very odd, the entire house was in darkness not one light showing from any of its many windows. Knowing how much Jan, hated the approach of night and the dark, and that the place was usually lit up like a ballroom, he was at once extremely concerned and said as much.

"Maybe there's been a power cut," Kate suggested, " It certainly it looks as if there has been enough snow here to bring power lines down."

"Oh Lord, I hope not," David replied, fumbling with his key ring to find the right key. "I've got candles in this bag, we realised yesterday we didn't have any, so I bought some lunchtime."

At last he managed to get the key into the lock, not an easy task for without the porch light to guide him it was extremely difficult to locate the lock. Turning the key at last he opened the door and they stumbled inside, to even denser darkness than outside.

Muffled sobbing met their entrance, alarmed David groped for the light switch by the door, checking to see, if indeed it was a power cut that had plunged the house into darkness. The switch wasn't even on and flicking it, light flooded the hall, dazzling them all for a few seconds.

In the corner, sitting on the floor huddled into the stairwell was Jan and the children.

* * * *

To the consternation of both, Jan appeared not to register their appearance; she continued sitting staring blankly before her. Her face was showing no emotion whatsoever, it was if her mind had retreated momentarily, to a place where no one and nothing could touch her, her face chalk white, her eyes dark ringed and with her long fair hair tangled around her face, she portrayed a picture of abject misery. Both the children were asleep in her arms, with tearstains on their cheeks.

It was a few seconds before she registered the fact of Kate's presence and in a strangled whisper, asked what she was doing there?

Spurred into action, David and Kate crossed the floor in seconds, David took the children from Jan, almost having to pry her arms from them, she was holding them so tightly, whilst Kate eased her to her feet and with a comforting arm around her thin shoulders, led her into the drawing room and settled her into the red armchair near the empty fireplace. She was undeniably shocked at the appalling change in her friend's appearance.

The house was freezing cold and when he came downstairs again, David checked the radiators and finding them barely warm he went to turn up the thermostat. Seeing it was already as high as it could go, he asked Kate to stay with Jan, whilst he went to the basement to check that the boiler had not gone out.

As he opened the door, cold damp air blew up from below, never a pleasant place at the best of times, David hurried down the steps and across the uneven stone flagged floor, to the wire cage against the back wall which housed the boiler, but he could see even as he reached the bottom step that it was still alight and was in fact roaring loudly as it was working so hard. He found an Allen key with which to bleed the radiators, thinking there was perhaps air in one or more of them, and that was the reason the heat was not getting through.

It took him some time to check on the radiators in all the rooms they were currently using but hoped the time it took, would allow Kate to make some headway with Jan. He had been naturally upset at finding Jan in such a distressed state, and hoped she would open up to Kate in a way she might not to him, in view of the tension between them of late. However as upset as he was, he couldn't help a degree of irritation in half expecting this to have been another of her episode of her playacting.

Kate meanwhile was trying to find out the cause of the upset, Jan was reluctant to speak at first and simply lay her head wearily on the arm of the chair. Kate patiently remained silent waiting for her to speak in her own time and at last Jan sat up and began recounting the evening's events.

'The night had been approaching, she'd said, she didn't want it to, she was frightened of the night, things that happened in the daylight were easier to bear. Paul had been difficult all day, for not only had he lost his beloved train but the cat had disappeared as well. With both children in tow, she had spent hours searching the house for both but there had been no sign of either. She had managed to overcome her panic attack that had hit her as soon as she stepped outside to look for the little cat, but had to give up the search soon after because of the encroaching darkness, she'd returned inside to prepare the evening meal, yet hours later the cat still had not returned, neither had Paul found his train.

She had been in the kitchen putting pizza and garlic bread into the oven, ready for their evening meal, when a figure had appeared in the room. Jan had not known whether it was a man or woman, for the figure had been wrapped in a dark hooded garment, the face concealed. The children had been in the drawing room, Sarah, safely in her playpen and Paul engrossed in the television, having momentarily forgotten about the missing cat and his beloved train.

Approaching her, the cloaked figure whoever or whatever it was, had with some invisible force slammed her across the room, as if she weighed no more than a feather? Then somehow, kept her motionless upon the floor where she had landed. Panic stricken, she had lain there unable to move panting for breath, watching helplessly as the figure had glided from the room towards her children.

It had seemed a very long time before she found she could breathe normally and could persuade her body to obey her will to move. Shaking, she had raised herself on all fours before pulling herself clumsily to her feet by the table. Sheer will power and the overwhelming protective instinct toward her children, had forced her to get up and face whatever threat was in her home.

The temperature had dropped dramatically and in amazement, she had seen that water dripping from the tap over the sink, had frozen solid. A sheet of ice had formed over the tiled floor and her rasping breath formed a white cloud, which hung in front of her face. Her hands were damp with fear- induced perspiration and her heart thudded painfully in her chest.

Shivering with cold, she had made her way unsteadily across the room, losing her balance more than once on the sheet of ice that still covered the floor. Entering the drawing room, she found the children as she had left them, blissfully unaware of anything untoward having taken place in the kitchen. Of the cloaked figure there had been no sign and the temperature in the drawing room was quite normal. Then as if all that had gone before hadn't been enough for her to contend with, the lights had gone out. Fumbling to find her way, she had managed to locate both children, who had been naturally terrified at being plunged into sudden darkness. Feeling her way with them both into the hall, she had crawled into the corner under the stairs and stayed there until she had been found, too frightened to come out.

Eventually both the children had cried themselves to sleep, which foolishly had left her feeling even more alone and vulnerable than ever.

"Oh Kate," she ended "such terrible things are happening here, frightening evil things, they just won't let me alone, David won't believe me or even begin to understand."

Wearily she laid her head again on the arm of the chair, silent tears rolling down her pale cheeks. Kate knelt on the floor before her, stroking her hair, deeply moved but for once totally unable to think of a single solitary thing to say that might comfort her.

David, having checked the radiators for air locks and finding none, returned and seated himself in his leather chair opposite the two women. He listened patiently whilst Kate repeated what Jan had told her, leading up to their finding them in the stairwell. Unable to think of anything to say with which to console Jan herself, she was looking to gain strength from him and maybe to find an answer.

Only when Kate had finished did Jan allow herself to glance at her husband, reluctantly seeing the familiar look of intense irritation upon his face. He said nothing to begin with merely shook his head but he made no move toward Jan to comfort her.

If he was entirely honest with himself, he did feel stirrings of guilt but he had let the moment pass, weeks ago when he might have reached across the widening gap and apologised to his wife.

Always having been able to confide in and rely on him in the past, these days Jan was aware of the huge void between them, she could sense his ever present impatience and wished, as she had so many times, that if he could only hear or see just one of the things she had, feeling that was all it would take for the whole situation between them to be resolved.

David's words, when he finally spoke stunned Kate, "Oh come on Jan you really cannot expect us to believe all this twaddle about ghosts and stuff, when is it going to end?" He got up from the chair, facing her with his eyes glaring angrily, on his face a cold vacant expression.

"If you could only see the things I do," Jan whispered.

"If you persist in this Jan, I won't be around to see anything," he paused, "I'll be damned if I'll up and leave this house, so you can stop acting out your little charade right now and make the best of things, it's no use you trying to win Kate over either, she won't be fooled any more than I am, you know something, you take the word actress to a whole new level." With that parting shot, he strode angrily from the room leaving the two women flabbergasted.

Kate couldn't believe his reaction, he and Jan had always been so close, yet there was a visible distance between them now that Kate had never expected to see. David had, it seemed not been at all prepared to give even the slightest credence to her story, looking upon this, the latest incident apparently one of many, as yet another fabrication of, as he saw it 'Jan's overactive imagination', hopefully strengthening her case to persuade him to give up his job and move. Up until now Kate would never have considered David a selfish person, but today she had seen him put his own desires before his concerns for his wife's happiness and well being.

Leaving Jan dissolving once again into tears, she ran after him, he was striding towards the stairs, his back to her as she called him.

"David, wait a moment please, can't we talk about this?"

With his foot already on the bottom stair, he turned.

"If you care anything for Jan, please try to understand that she is frightened and unhappy, desperately unhappy, that much is obvious."

David opened his mouth to say something, though better of it and appeared to be thinking of something else to say.

"I just can't believe that someone as intelligent as I've always thought Jan to be would think this house is haunted."

"Well perhaps you should consider that it might be, just because you haven't seen anything so far, doesn't mean that you won't, after all by your own admission you are hardly ever here"

"There are no such things as ghosts Kate, I have never believed in that supernatural stuff; I'm only interested in things than can be scientifically proved."

"Yes but what if you're wrong?" she persisted stubbornly.

"Oh I've had enough of this, I'm sorry Kate, its good of you to defend her but I still believe it to be a ploy, she hates this house and would do anything to move out of it, I refuse to give in to her," and with that he ran up the stairs.

CHAPTER 10

In spite of having Kate for company, the next few days were extremely difficult for Jan. The close relationship the two women had shared appeared to have altered. In the past, they had always been able to talk to each about anything, now, it wasn't that they couldn't talk any more exactly, but rather that Jan was on guard all the time, feeling that Kate and David were forming an alliance behind her back. Twice she had come upon them talking earnestly to each other, conversation which had ceased the moment she had entered the room and later when she had dared to ask her husband what the two of them had been discussing he had grown angry.

"For goodness sake Jan, heavens knows I need someone to talk to," he had railed, "All you go on and on about is the strange things you see and hear, when I know darn well it is all a stupid ploy on your part to persuade me to move back to London."

"We've already had this conversation David."

"Well we're having it again," he spat.

"Well this time I am not going to be a part of it," Jan argued back striding angrily from the room.

She sat rigidly at the kitchen table aware that she was terrified of her own house, yet knowing that her husband went about his days in rapture. She knew that David would be sitting in his chair waiting for her to apologise, wearing the hurt look she was coming to know so well. Well he would have to wait; she was damned if she would lie and say that she had made it all up."

There had been no further 'ghostly' incidents since Kate's arrival, making things look even worse for Jan's credibility, as if David needed further convincing, that it was all in his wife's mind, or worse still a carefully contrived plot to force him to return them to the city.

Since, she had been staying with them, Jan had noticed something odd about Kate that concerned her greatly. She noticed that she didn't appear to enjoy being around the children as much as she had used to, it was as if more than a couple of hours in their company, and it became too much and she would take herself off and walk around the grounds. Once, Jan even heard her tell Paul to go away and leave her in peace, Jan had felt indignant on her son's behalf, knowing how fond he was of Kate. It simply wasn't like Kate at all, any more than it was like David to act the way he had of late, it was, and she thought wildly, as if something in the house were changing their personalities, heaven knew it had changed hers, for she had become a nervous wreck. There was, without doubt something menacing in Challoners, strange and horrifying, threatening everything she held dear.

A couple of days later, David returned home from the office in extremely good spirits and informed Jan he had been awarded a bonus. He asked if she would like to be taken out for a celebration meal the next day, if Kate would agree to baby- sit. Jan was surprised and relieved, as vague signs of the husband she knew and loved appeared to be re-emerging. He told her, that he had it on good authority from colleagues in the office, that the 'Green Man' in Lesser Kirston, did an excellent steak and in view of the fact that the weather had not improved, decided it would be sensible to travel no further than the village to eat, in any event.

Jan found her spirits soaring; thinking that perhaps David was attempting to make things up to her, for the way he had behaved of late. The agoraphobia bothered her but she knew that if she could make into the confines of the car and from there into the Pub without too much exposure to the outdoors, she was sure she would be able to manage. She was rather hurt though that David hadn't thought to ask if going out might be a problem for her.

Waiting until Kate was out of the room one evening, she put her arms around him and whispered, "what's happening to us, we used to be so happy together?" he pulled away sharply as if unable to bear her touch saying, "What's happening to you, don't you mean? You're the one who has changed Jan, he turned his back to her, "all you ever talk about these days is the snow, the whispers, the apparitions, honestly Jan you should hear yourself sometimes, it drives me mad, oh and of course the agoraphobia, as well, mustn't forget that must we?" He paused. "You seem to have totally lost the art of interesting conversation. It's a good job Kate's here. At least she has something interesting to talk about."

Her happy mood of earlier quite ruined, Jan left the room struggling to hold back the tears, which threatened to fall only too easily these days. She was also undeniably jealous of her best friend, for the fact that these days David seemed to prefer to spend his time with her.

When told of the proposed outing, Kate agreed readily to mind the children, although it gave Jan a niggling worry that she might lose her patience when left on her own with them. She wasn't concerned with regard to leaving them with Kate as far as the supernatural 'incidents' were concerned, as all the things that were happening appeared only to happen to her anyway, for once her main concern was nothing to do with her home.

Dismissing it as being paranoid, she manages to summon up some enthusiasm for her dinner out with her husband, it would be the first time she had left Challoners, since they moved in. David always having been too busy or tired to take her until now, and anyway most weekends he had worked. Ironic that the first weekend he should have taken off had been when Kate arrived.

Jan had already; lay out on her bed, the clothes she had decided to wear. In the mood to dress up a little, she had chosen her best 'little black dress' with a its plunging neckline, hoping it would not give people in the village too much of a cultural shock, feeling that perhaps they didn't dress up too much in Lesser Kirston.

Thinking back to the day they had driven through the village for the first time, all she remembered about the one or two women she had seen on the street, were that they had all worn headscarves, reminding her of the women in Croatia, where she and David had once taken a holiday. Another 'trade mark' of village life had appeared to be the essential shopping basket looped over their arms.

* * * *

The morning of the proposed evening out, Kate surprised Jan by suggesting that they go and walk by the lake and talk for a while.

"Must we, you know I hate the woods?" Jan protested, "added to that, I know another panic attack will begin the minute I set foot outside, "she shivered at the thought.

"You'll never overcome your fear of the woods if you stay away," Kate sensibly told her, "confrontation is the most effective way of dealing with fear. Similarly, you must learn to overcome and control the panic attacks, if you expect them to happen then of course they will, your mind having been conditioned to expect them.

Although Jan knew that there was some truth in what Kate was saying, she felt resentment towards her. She knew that Kate had never experienced a panic attack personally and felt she wouldn't be so self-righteous if she had; it was a dreadfully frightening experience.

Another bitterly cold day, the clouds were speeding across the sky angrily, for the wind was high, so warmly wrapped up with Sarah in the carrier on Jan's back and Paul skipping happily alongside, they set off making their way across the lawn, their feet crunching in what remained of the frozen snow.

As they had left the house Jan had hovered nervously on the doorstep, feeling the familiar tightening in her chest and her heartbeat increasing to frightening speed as she panted for breath, contemplating the first step outside, fighting to control it, incredibly it began to ease.

The two women spoke little as they made their way toward the woods, listening instead to Paul's idle chatter. Although it gave no warmth, a watery sun shone for the first time for many days and the icicles hanging from the eaves were beginning to drip, indicating a thaw had set in. The blue-black branches of the oaks, stood out in stark relief against the faded blue of the winter sky, casting faint shadows across the lawn in the weak sunlight.

Comfortingly, a little of the old camaraderie between the two women, returned that day and they laughed as they watched Paul race through the woods kicking up leaves delightedly. Growing tired, he began collecting twigs, with which he informed them very seriously, he was going to build something when he got home.

Reaching the lake at last, they skirted around bushes and vines still silvered with frost, not yet dispelled by the weak sunlight. Reaching a pebble outcrop with a scattering of large rocks, they began to talk, much more so than they had done in the last few days.

Paul occupied himself by throwing pebbles on to the frozen lake, the ice was thinning and water lapped gently at the edges, a comforting sound. Here, where the trees grew less densely and she could see a large expanse of sky, Jan felt marginally more at ease. She looked across the frozen lake thinking how the whole scene looked quite unearthly beautiful covered in snow.

Kate spoke first, "It must be gorgeous here in the summertime, I can see it now with trees with leaves that bright fresh green when they are new, sunlight dancing on the water and dragonflies hovering amongst the rushes. I wonder if it is possible to swim in the lake, is it very deep?"

"I've no idea, " Jan spoke absent-mindedly for try as she might she could see the lake no other way that it was today, her imagination would not let her, her mind was too full of other things, things she wanted to get off her chest.

"It isn't my imagination you know," she went on quietly, having made sure that Paul was out of earshot. "Kate tell me honestly, haven't you seen or heard a single thing that you could interpret as strange since you've been here? Her voice was pleading.

Kate sighed heavily and kicked despondently at the shingle, with the toe of her elegant black leather boot.

"I wish I could say I had Jan," she muttered in reply, "but I have to be honest, I feel more relaxed and comfortable at Challoners than I have ever felt anywhere, well that is I would do apart from..." she hesitated, reluctant to speak the words that had already formed in her mind.

"Apart from the discord between David and myself do you mean?" asked Jan guessing correctly the reason for her friend's obvious reluctance to continue.

"Well you have to admit that it is so unlike you both."

"Would you think me unhinged, if I told you that I believe it is the influence of some evil force in the house that is causing the change in David?" Jan said her dark eyes fixed pleadingly on Kate's face.

"Jan, I really don't know anything about the supernatural, " Kate confessed, "I only know that as far as I am concerned, Challoners is a beautiful house, steeped in history, peaceful and not at all threatening in any way, shape or form. Don't you think that perhaps you have blown things out of proportion, and it is having a snowball effect?"

Jan sighed helplessly, she had hoped that away from the house she might have been able to convince Kate that there were things happening here in Challoners, that were unnatural and totally out of control, but saw now that it was as impossible, as trying to convince her husband had been.

"You are going to lose David through all this you know if you're not careful," Kate warned, averting her gaze from Jan's face, "even I can see that he's reaching the end of his patience and sympathy."

"What patience and sympathy?" Jan retorted bitterly, "he's never had any, not where this matter is concerned."

Kate's mind was in turmoil, she should she knew be taking a greater stand of support for her friend, yet, as was David, she too was beginning to feel irritated and annoyed at Jan's dogmatic persistence in keeping this fiasco going. Surely if indeed the house really was haunted, one of them, herself, David or even Paul would have felt, seen or commented on something? The very fact that they hadn't was highly suspect. She had been alarmed at the change in Jan's appearance when she had arrived, seeing that her friend had visibly lost weight and was far from happy, however now felt sure that the reason was homesickness for her old life in London that was causing it, nothing more.

More and more she found herself taking David's view, in that Jan had hatched up the whole thing, cleverly though, she had to admit, for the Jan she knew of old, could never have conceived of such an idea.

She also felt more than a little anger towards her for the fact that her friend was not more appreciative of the wonderful life she had and guiltily she found herself even envying Jan her marriage. She pulled herself up short, forced to examine her feelings, she wondered if it was sympathy she felt for him in this bizarre situation or something more. She had always found him attractive God knew, and sexually appealing, but being her best friend's husband, had put him firmly out of bounds of course. Now things were beginning to look different, she knew that David was attracted to her he had made that obvious. A deep surge of guilt swept uncomfortably over her as Jan glanced at her and smiled, she wouldn't be smiling if she had any idea, of the thoughts coursing through Kate's mind at that moment.

They had returned to the house and once inside Kate followed Jan into the kitchen reluctant to let the subject drop.

"Come on Jan you can confide in me, there isn't really anything going on here is there? It's all a plan to persuade David to move back to London isn't it? "

Jan was livid, her fragile calm snapping at last.

"How dare you," she spat," how could you even think that of me Kate, you who know me so well?"

Taken aback at her outburst, Kate retorted, "Honestly Jan, you must think we are idiots, it's as plain as plain can be, that the only things going on are in your disturbed mind." With that she swept regally out of the room having decided a shower may calm her down.

Jan stood motionless looking out of the kitchen window, seeing nothing lost in thought. It was the first real argument she could ever remember having with Kate and it didn't sit well with her.

There was little doubt that of the two of them, Kate was the stronger personality and for the first time nagging little doubts crept into Jan's mind, about how much of a friend Kate had actually been to her in the past. Was this the first row they'd had simply because it was the first time that she had actually stood up to Kate and defended herself in any given situation? If she was entirely honest with herself, from the time they had met, she had lived in Kate's shadow, Kate always being the vivacious extrovert, the one with stunning looks and significant talent, whilst she Jan, had meekly tagged along, grateful for her company.

Her reminiscing brought into her mind many memories she had thought long forgotten, her mind wandered back to growing up with her Mum and Dad in the modest little semi detached house in Bromley in Kent.

She had met Kate for the first time in *The Crooked Steeple*, a pub on the outskirts of town. A modern building with no character it had little to recommend it other than it was fairly central and attracted a great deal of people working in and around Bromley centre.

After leaving College, Jan had been thrilled to land her first job as a receptionist in a hairdressing Salon. One evening, a few days after she had started, one of the girls she worked with asked her if she would like to join her and a few friends for a drink at *The Crooked Steeple*.

They had been a rowdy lot and Jan, being quite introverted, had hung back at the edge of the crowd. Feeling ignored and very much out of place, she had excused herself and gone to the ladies and found herself washing her hands at the basin, next to a pretty dark haired girl who had caught her eye and smiled at her in the mirror.

That had been the beginning of their friendship, the girl being Kate and they had spent the rest of the evening together chatting. Kate had been in the pub alone, a fact that had made Jan envious to begin with, for she would never have had the self-assurance to go into a pub alone. Kate positively breathed self-assurance, for her clothes and make up were always impeccable, her shoes and handbags made of the softest leather always bore designer labels.

Over the next few weeks, they had met up several times and she had found out quite a lot about her new friend. Kate, short for Katrina was at that time living in Lewisham in an imposing detached house with her father. As her Mother had died when she was twelve, her father, a wealthy merchant banker had hired a nanny to take care of her due to the fact that he had to spend so much time abroad. Although she lacked a mother, Kate wanted for nothing else and was completely indulged in whatever she wanted to own or do.

The difference in their backgrounds had appeared to have no effect on their friendship. Jan assumed that because she was shy and in her opinion, only average looking, she had been a perfect foil for Kate's dark vivacious beauty and lively personality.

It had been Kate who had introduced her to David, when one evening on her own date she had suggested Jan come along to make up a foursome.

She remembered the night she had met David so well, she was very shy with him at first, greatly impressed with his obvious charm, she had taken to him immediately, and he was extraordinarily good looking with blue eyes, lean frame and solid square shoulders. Appearing quietly sure of himself, to Jan he was perfection itself, a vivid contrast from any of the boyfriends she had been out with in the past, not that there had been very many. The evening was a success even although Kate flirted outrageously throughout with David to the extent that Jan had half expected Kate's date to protest, but he apparently was quite used to it, turning a blind eye.

When David had smiled at her, Jan had felt a vivid flush explode upon her face and her heart quicken. At the end of an evening, which had been the happiest she could remember spending in a long while, she had held out her hand formally when they said goodnight, David had taken it but leaned forward and lightly brushed her lips with his own.

It had been a source of amazement to her that David appeared to be as attracted to her as she was to him, for privately she had thought Kate was far more the type of girl he would be interested in. David had been in his last year at University as a mature student, graduation day was rapidly approaching and Jan was pleased to able to share his great day with him. She had stood in the great hall and watched him receive his diploma, knowing that his path toward that moment had not been easy. He'd had no parents to fund him and had scraped by on a pittance earned from any menial job he could find, which would pay his fees. Cloaked in cap and gown and holding his diploma he had posed for the obligatory graduation photograph, how proud she had been to have shared that moment with him.

She had been so caught up in the excitement of the day, she remembered, that she had found herself wishing that her own life had taken a similar path and that she had studied harder and been given the chance to attend University and she voiced her feelings to David as they sat in the campus restaurant over a cup of coffee. He had patted her hand across the table smiling and said, "Yes but look around you Jan, hundreds of people have graduated today, but it is a sad fact of life that a year down the line from now, a good quarter of them will still be without a job due to being overqualified. It is not enough to have a University background and a degree; sometimes experience of life itself counts for just as much."

David, luckily had not been among the quarter he'd mentioned and had begun working almost immediately at Carforth's laboratories as a technician, quickly advancing, making their marriage a year later possible.

Kate's father had given Kate a flat in the city on her eighteenth birthday, a gesture, which had made Jan feel childish for still living at home with her parents. Although Kate herself had not suggested Jan move in and share her own flat, she had put her in touch with a friend of hers who was looking for a flat mate, so it had transpired that Jan had moved in with Carly, two years her senior and a student at Art College. Far from being a struggling student though, Carly also was financed by her parents who had paid for the flat the two of them shared.

Jan had found it vastly different from living at home and relished in her newfound independence. For one thing there was no one to constantly berate her if her room was untidy, Carly being if anything, even untidier. In the flat, no one cared or commented if things were left scattered on the floor, no one picked up the records tossed across her bed or complained at the outrageous psychedelic posters that decorated her walls. Clothes were hung on every available surface and shoes left where they were kicked off.

That all changed as the relationship with David developed further and he began coming back to the flat, gradually she reverted to the habits her mother had instilled upon her for in truth Jan hated disorder and disarray. If Carly was irritated by the fact that Jan was constantly clearing up after her, she made no mention of it, she was an easygoing girl, and little ruffled her feathers.

Jan had always found it a mystery that Kate had never married, the last thing she would have ever expected, was that of the two of them, she herself would be the first to take the plunge. She did wonder sometimes whether it could be that Kate was rather too particular, or simply that the right man hadn't yet entered her life.

Kate liked to have her own way it was true, many times she, Jan had suggested a film she would like to see when they went to the Cinema together, now, she found herself remembering that Kate had always given some reason for not wanting to see it, preferring another and Jan, being Jan, always gave in without reproach. There had, she realised been countless incidents when she had given way to Kate's whims over her own desires.

Tearing her thoughts back to the present, she saw again the snowy scene lay out before her, was there anything more forbidding than this desolate house in this frozen wintry scene she wondered? Wrenching her eyes away she looked around the room 'what secrets are you hiding?' she muttered to the house in general and almost expected some kind of reply.

* * * *

Lunch over, Kate asked Jan again, if she would show her the attics, Jan had always put her off when she had mentioned the attics before, this time however, she agreed, albeit reluctantly and asked Paul if he would like to accompany them. He refused, saying he wanted to play in his room with the sticks he'd collected, using them to build a bridge for his train, ready for when it turned up again.

Kate, it appeared, had either forgotten the outburst earlier on or wanted to pretend it hadn't happened, either way Jan was relieved for in spite of everything she hated to fall out with anyone, and uncomfortable atmospheres between people made her feel physically sick.

Kate offered to put Sarah into her cot for her nap, so Jan went on up the stairs ahead of her, gritting her teeth as she passed the 'cold spot', which was always waiting for her as she approached the top stair. She heard her name called again louder than ever before, she ignored it, knowing it was useless to mention it to Kate for she wouldn't be able to hear it.

Reaching the strange little attic door, so unlike all the others in the house, she went to open it but found she was unable to. She pulled harder thinking it was perhaps sticking in the frame, but it stubbornly refused to budge and she was still persistently tugging at it when Kate joined her.

"Perhaps it's locked," she said.

"But I've never locked it, I don't even know if there is a key for it."

"Where do you keep your keys?" Kate asked.

"In the kitchen, on a hook in the broom cupboard, next to the electricity meter."

"I'll go and look if you like. I wonder what sort of key it is?"

They looked closely at the lock.

"Ah," Kate said "that should be easy it's a mortice lock, all your other locks are Yale aren't they?" Jan nodded her confirmation.

"Okay." Kate ran off along the landing and down the stairs to see what she could find, calling something to Paul as she passed his room, Jan heard him giggle in response.

Still convinced that the door couldn't be locked, Jan persisted in her efforts to get it open. Having no success, she gave up trying and wandered over to the window, leaning heavily on the stone sill. The atmosphere was oppressive, she felt as if the house around her was forcing her spirits down to a point where she could no longer find the energy to get them back up again. Forcing the feeling from her mind, she took in the winter landscape; it was such a clear day that even the hills of Snowdonia in the far distance were plainly visible, with their 'icing' of snow.

A draught brushed her legs and turning to see where it could have come from, she saw to her surprise that the attic door was standing wide open and she was sure she could hear light footsteps running up the spiral stairway behind it.

She put a hand out, but before she could grasp the handle, the door swung sharply away from her, slamming shut with a loud bang. Opening just a little again, it then closed, then opened, and then closed, repeating this over and over again, faster and faster.

Along the corridor Paul played on oblivious, seemingly unable to hear the constant banging taking place just yards from his room. Bombarded by that hateful voice calling her name over and over again, in accompaniment with the continuous banging of the door,

Jan sank down on the landing floor with her hands over her ears, which was where Kate found her a few minutes later.

CHAPTER 11

"Are you sure you didn't see anything, anything at all?" David persisted, the next morning.

"No, not a thing, the door was closed, the way it had been when I went to look for a key." Kate assured him.

David paced the room angrily, for he had returned from work the night before, to find Jan in another of her 'states' as he was beginning to address her so called 'sightings'. She had been so utterly distressed, that the plans for the much looked forward to evening out at the pub for a meal, had been abandoned. Having no telephone, it had been necessary for David to drive to the village to cancel the table and make apologies for the lateness of the cancellation, explaining that his wife was not feeling well; he had been far from pleased.

* * * *

Jan wandered into the room, having left the children finishing their breakfast in the kitchen.

David, sitting across from Kate, gave his wife a cursory glance and without speaking got up and left the room.

Visibly snubbed before her friend, Jan lowered her eyes. Kate felt distinctly uncomfortable, these last few days, had shown her that Jan's 'imaginings', for Kate was now convinced that, that was what they were, had carved a rift in their friendship, which was proving difficult to close. The uneasy and volatile tension between Jan and David, was bringing her down. This morning she had awoken with a Migraine, which although mild in intensity and now abating, was something she had not suffered for a long time, she had to leave, she was doing no good here it was obvious.

She leaned across the table and rested her hand on Jan's. Hesitantly, for she did rather feel she was abandoning her friend at a time of need, she explained that she felt the time had come for her to return to London. Jan was acutely embarrassed; knowing the reason without doubt, was the continuously strained atmosphere between David and herself.

"Won't you at least stay until the weather improves?" she urged half-heartedly knowing already what Kate's answer would be.

"No I'd better not, it might be days yet before the snow has gone and I did say I could only stay a short time, I'll be leaving first thing in the morning"

They got through the day somehow, although the atmosphere remained tense, it didn't take long for the children to pick up the vibes resulting in them both being irritable and impossible to please. Jan was more than relieved when the time came to put them to bed, for she had developed a throbbing headache and was feeling mentally and physically drained. She decided to go and lie down herself, leaving Kate watching the television. Before she went up, she put David's meal into the microwave, for once Jan was not going to wait up for him, feeling he had Kate for company after all.

Jan slept reasonably well that night for once and woke feeling refreshed, she went down stairs after checking the children were still sleeping and made herself a cup of coffee, taking it into the drawing room she curled up in the red velvet chair. Oddly, she began to feel very drowsy again and found herself dozing off. She half sensed someone entering the room but as she flicked open her eyes to see whom it was, it appeared they had gone, dozing off again she had a nightmare and woke with a start, perspiring.

She needed to take a shower; the house was quiet so she knew the children must still been sleeping, as must also be David and Kate. She didn't want to disturb David by using the shower in their en suite and Kate had her own bathroom attached to the guest room she was occupying, so Jan chose to use the bathroom with the flowered fittings, knowing it wouldn't disturb anyone. She hurried past the 'cold spot' on the stairs hearing the familiar whispering begin again. Ignoring it, she made her way to the bathroom. Just as she put her hand out to grasp the handle she heard muffled voices inside, confusing them with the whispering she could also hear she opened the door. The scene before her filled her with horror chilling her to the bone, but it was not supernatural this time, David and Kate were inside; neither of them had heard the door open for quite obviously they had other things on their mind. David was already naked and he was at that moment, gently slipping Kate's red satin robe from her shoulders.

With heart pounding, Jan closed the door covering her mouth with her hand, she stood as if frozen to the spot leaning on the doorjamb, unable to think let alone move. She couldn't begin to take in what she had witnessed, never in her wildest dreams had she imagined that David and Kate... it was quite unthinkable.

Eventually she forced herself to move away from the door, unable to bear listening any longer to the obvious sounds of her husband and best friend making love in her home. She knew she should have confronted them but couldn't bring herself to do so, she hadn't the strength and she needed to think. She lurched downstairs and sat at the kitchen table, surprisingly she found she couldn't cry, that would come later, just for now the hurt went far too deep.

She wasn't sure how long she had sat there, when she heard Sarah begin to cry, woodenly she rose to her feet and automatically climbed the stairs to fetch her, it would be just too bad if David and Kate chose this moment to let themselves out of the bathroom and came face to face with her, they must have known it would be a possibility. All was quiet apart from Sarah however and glancing through her own bedroom door as she passed, Jan was astonished to see David fast asleep in bed. Unable to resist, she glanced into Kate's room as well, she also was soundly sleeping still, and surely she hadn't imagined what she had seen in the bathroom, had she? Now she was even beginning to doubt herself.

Ignoring Sarah's cries for the moment, Jan went into the bathroom, it was a neat as it always was, no signs of anyone having been there at all. Could it have been another illusion brought about by whatever evil filled this house? Jan just wasn't sure anymore.

True to her word Kate made preparations to leave that morning, Jan stood watching from the doorway as she bundled her things together without her usual attention to neatly folding each item as it was packed, so anxious was she to leave without delay.

Jan felt she must try once again to re establish her position with Kate.

"I just don't understand what is wrong with David, she said, "He's never doubted me before."

Kate paused in her packing and shifted uncomfortably, Jan knew it was because she had divided loyalties, she bit her lip reluctant to continue but needing to never the less.

"I get so angry," she said, "he's my husband, and he should support me at all times."

Kate looked up, a shadow crossing her face, she signalled to Jan with her eyes.

Jan turned

David had come up behind her and was looking furious, having overheard her last words.

"*You* get angry," he said, "how on earth do you think I feel? As for supporting you, would you support me if I constantly spoke about wild fantasies there was no proof of or foundation for, I think not, you ask for everything you get," turning he strode angrily away.

Jan could say no more, she had toyed with telling Kate of what she had seen in the bathroom earlier, but still doubted her own eyes. If it had been yet another illusion, Jan would feel bereft for although things had changed between them, she still considered Kate her best friend and would miss her company.

David left for work at the same time, following Kate's car slowly out of the drive, the tyres crunching over the frozen snow. The promised thaw having come to nothing, several nights of severe frost had left the ground, dangerously slippery again. Jan watched their departure with a heavy heart, feeling she had lost something special. She was more than ever convinced that the house and its restless spirits were responsible for everything that was turning sour in her life.

Just before lunch, a van drove into the drive and pulled up, it was the telephone engineer, with all that had been going on over the past few days Jan had quite forgotten he was coming, even David had not remembered. She was pathetically thrilled to see him, knowing his presence meant she would be in touch with the outside world again for a little while.

Before he had arrived, it had been an extremely difficult morning for Jan; she'd tried very hard to put the uncomfortable feelings of having lost a long-standing friend, to one side in busying herself about the house. Emptying the dishwasher machine, she put away the dishes and after closing the cupboards, wiped down the draining board before moving on to fetch the laundry from the utility room. As she left the room a series of loud bangs caused her to look back into the kitchen, to her amazement, every single cupboard door in the kitchen stood wide open. Nervously she returned and closed them but as she made to leave the room once more they all flew open again, as if in sheer defiance.

This time she left them as they were.

The whispering was non-stop, footsteps tramped relentlessly back and forth in some room or other above her head and the presence she felt behind her was there almost constantly. The spirits in the house knew that any possible ally she might have had in Kate had now gone and that in doing so, had left her wide open to further attack.

The Engineer explained to her that the new underground cables had been laid, and that all he was required to do, was to connect a box to the wall outside and run the wires through to wherever she wanted the telephone and the various extensions to be situated.

Jan thought quickly, for some reason David and she had not discussed where the phones were to be placed. She decided that logically of course, the main one should be in the hall, with an extension in their bedroom, another in the kitchen and a third in the small bedroom next to the attic door that David had decided to use as a study.

Little Paul watched in fascination, as the engineer carried in reels of cable, handsets and a large box of tools. Depositing them on the hall floor, he winked at Paul and asked him to keep an eye on them whilst he went to fix the connection box to the wall outside. The next few minutes were filled with the sound of drilling as the engineer made the hole for the wires to pass through. Even that sound however did not drown out the persistent whispering.

Crossing the hall to the kitchen to make the engineer a cup of tea, Jan caught sight of her reflection in the mirror above the telephone table and was shocked at her appearance. Her now sallow skin appeared to have 'shrunk' for her cheekbones stood out sharply, emphasizing the dark rings around her eyes. The main reason for her gaunt appearance, she felt, was not only her growing fear of Challoners and the spirits she knew it housed, but also severe sleep deprivation. Forever since the 'funeral party' manifestation, what sleep she was able to grasp was shallow and unsatisfactory. She slept most night with her head buried deep beneath the Duvet, afraid to look out for fear of what she might see. During the time between wakefulness and dozing, her thoughts and imagination ran riot, her body racked with chronic fatigue. It had become normal, in the depths of the night when David and her babies slept soundly, for her to toss and turn ever watchful for something materialising before her or listening again for that maddeningly familiar voice calling her name over and over again.

She had tried sitting up really late watching television, in an effort to tire her herself completely, but found she was taking in nothing, of the programmes played out before her.

David and she were growing further and further apart, a chasm between them that she seemed unable to cross, which worried her as much as the 'haunting'. He would go to bed at his usual time, too tired to sit up with her and by the time she crawled in beside him, he was sleeping deeply. They hardly talked at all any more and Jan was dreadfully lonely.

After each restless night she would reluctantly drag herself out of bed dreading the day before her. This house and its evil were slowly and systematically destroying her health and marriage.

Interrupting her reverie, the engineer came back inside the hall.

"I'm sorry Mrs Blake, I'm not going to be able to finish up, I have to go back to the depot, as I seem to be missing a connector I need." He smiled apologetically, "the only thing is, it's going to take me a good hour to get there and back and I have another job booked in Milborough for this afternoon."

Seeing the look of blatant disappointment she was unable to hide, he continued, "I will do my best to get back today, it just depends on how straight forward the other job turns out to be. If not it may be a day or so I'm afraid, I have a lot of work on at the moment."

Foolishly, for a bizarre moment, Jan wanted to reach out and hold the man, to put her in touch with reality. Collecting herself and smiling weakly she said, "Of course, don't worry I know you'll do what you can." The engineer then gathered up his tools, stacked the coils of cable and the handsets neatly beneath the hall table, said 'goodbye' to Paul and took his leave.

Each time she passed the coil of wire and handsets, the inanimate objects mocked Jan, as if to say, 'so near and yet so far,' to being in touch with the outside world again.

* * * *

She set about preparing the children some soup for lunch, turning on the radio whilst she waited for it to warm through, but as always happened lately, after just a few minutes there was so much static she had no alternative but to switch it off again. Her stomach felt empty, she had never felt so low, so utterly miserable that it bordered on illness. If only the voices would stop, she heard them everywhere, constant and incessant, never distinct enough to be understood. She'd begun to hate the sound of her own name as it was repeatedly called.

The aroma from the heating soup, sickened her to the point of nausea, and she shivered as the temperature in the room suddenly plummeted.

'Oh no not again', she thought. A touch on her shoulder caused her to whirl, prickles dancing coldly down her spine, when as usual there was nothing there.

'Of course there isn't,' she muttered bitterly, 'there never is'. The whispering around her increased and at once felt she could stand it no more.

"What do you want from me?" She screamed as she swept from the room to find the children, slamming the door behind her, as if it wouldn't follow through the closed door haunting her every breathing moment.

* * * *

Most evenings after the children had been put to bed, Jan would turn on the television just for background noise until David came home. Tonight she hadn't for some reason and wandering into the kitchen, it struck her suddenly how very quiet it was.

Of course it should have been, apart from the hum of the refrigerator and the ticking of the kitchen wall clock, but something was wrong, something was missing.

With a shock she realised that the constant whispering, which was always with her these days had stopped. She gave a nervous little giggle and at once raised her hand to her mouth to stifle the sound. She was almost afraid to breathe in case she started it off again. She looked tentatively around her, over her shoulder towards the hall and back again, sweeping the kitchen with her gaze. All seemed normal, too normal, a word she had thought never to use again in connection with Challoners.

Exhilaration and excitement bubbled up inside her, but too soon, she should have known it was a trick, merely a brief respite before the next onslaught. For the next moment an overwhelming tide of evil surrounded her, extinguishing her moment of relief, as effectively as a bucket of water thrown over a flame.

Something terrible she knew, was about to happen and it didn't let her down.

A deafening noise filled the air, roaring like thunder as a dark shadow swept across the kitchen above her. Incredibly a huge shapeless mass was shifting, undulating and forming an obnoxious cloud around her. Finding her voice, she screamed, extending her arms as if in an effort to push it away from her. It settled on and around her, an icy cold blanket. The last thing she thought she saw was ghostly hand reaching out from the dark to encircle her throat.

* * * *

Jan opened her eyes to find herself prostrate upon the kitchen floor. The cold light of the winter morning was showing through the window, which was open wide and slamming back and forth against the wall. The gale howling outside blew fiercely through the gap causing the curtains to flap wildly against the walls. She thought it was a miracle she hadn't died of exposure for she was so cold that she was unable to stop shivering. Her head felt curiously vacant and for a few moments she was entirely incapable of action. As she began to feel her strength returning, she grasped the table leg for support to pull herself gradually to her feet. Holding on weakly until she felt she could place one foot before the other confidently. At that moment, her gaze flickered over the clock on the wall. How could it be, it was 9a.m., had she really lay there all night?

As full awareness returned, so it appeared, did normality. The window was no longer open, when had it closed? The curtains hung down in neat folds, the blind behind them undisturbed. She heard the familiar rattle of the old radiators as the heating came on and the room gradually grew warmer.

An annoying thought was mulling around at the back of her fuzzy mind, one that troubled her. Finally she brought it to the surface, why had David not found her? She couldn't even remember him coming home, although of course he must have done. Pulling herself shakily to her feet, she grabbed the corner of the table to steady herself, as a wave of nauseating dizziness swept over her.

After waiting for a few moments, she ventured toward the door; she could hear Sarah begin to cry. Making her way up the stairs as quickly as her swimming head would allow, she heard Paul talking to his little sister.

"It's all right Sarah. Mummy will be coming in a minute. I'll go and find her for you."

He bounded out of the door and met his Mother at the top of the stairs, just after she had passed through the familiar 'cold spot'.

"Where were you Mummy?" he asked.

"I was downstairs, why didn't you ask Daddy to see to Sarah?"

"Because he's not here of course," said the little boy looking quizzically at her, as if she should have known that anyway.

"What do you mean he isn't here?" Jan was confused; she felt she would be able to make more sense of what Paul was saying if only her throbbing head would let her.

She took his hand and walked quickly into her and David's room. Paul was quite right, David wasn't there and the bed had not been slept in.

How Jan managed to keep going that morning she really had no idea, she could only assume that once again her body had switched to an automatic mode, needing to do so for the sake of taking care of her children.

Stiff and sore from the night on the kitchen floor, she wondered if she could grab a quick bath to warm herself up. Sarah was in her playpen in the drawing room with Paul playing nearby. With a start she noticed he was playing with his train, the one they had spent hours looking for and was even now, pushing it around the track he'd set up.

"You've found your train Paul, where was it?

"Paul jumped up laughing.

"You know Mummy, you hid it didn't you?"

"No I.....why where did you find it?" she stopped herself quickly waiting to see what he was going to say.

"I found it in the attic."

"In the attic?" Paul, you know I told you never to go up there."

"I only went cos I heard you up there Mummy. I heard you walking about when I woke up. I went to look, but you must have come down without me hearing you. Anyway, I found my train. You are naughty mummy, you shouldn't have hidden it." His little face wrinkled up in a frown, as he tried to understand why his Mother would have let him get so upset about the train, when she knew where it was all the time.

Jan swallowed; she didn't have the first idea what to say to him, without letting him know that abnormal forces must have moved his train to the attic.

Paul, saved her further explanation, having noticed that Sarah had a little arm extended out of the bars of the playpen and was pulling apart the track he had set up so carefully. He hurried back to move it out of her reach, all else forgotten for the time being.

"I'm just going to take a very quick bath," Jan told him, "Call if you need anything and I'll come straight away."

Paul nodded and returned to his game, Sarah watching intently.

Jan hurried into the bathroom and turned on the taps. When the bath was full she pulled her long hair back into a pony tail and wound it on top of her head, securing it with a couple of pins from the glass bowl on the Vanity unit. She wearily dragged off her clothes, then careful to leave the door ajar so she might hear if the children called, she climbed into the deep bath, lowering herself into the water and easing herself as flat as it was possible to lie, resting her head on the back shelf. She closed her eyes luxuriating in the warmth, which spread throughout her tired chilled body.

A droning sound broke the silence forcing her to open her eyes. Surely it couldn't be a bee in the middle of winter?

In the centre of the room, hovering close to the ceiling was a small ball of fire rotating slowly, from it came the sound she had heard. Sitting bolt up right in the bath, the air around her exploded and the water in the bath began to ice over. Jan scrambled to get out feeling the sharp ice slash her leg, as she dragged it hastily over the side of the bath, leaving a trail of blood of the flowered surface.

Searing heat emanated from the fireball as it dived and darted around the room, always somehow managing to be between her and the door if she tried to escape. Once or twice it came so close, she could smell her hair singeing.

A bolt of lightning lit up the room from outside, although no thunder followed. Jan was flung to the wall furthest from the door, the towel she had managed to wrap around her, biting tightly into the skin beneath her arms.

Whispers, moans, screams, rose up around her filling the air with a cacophony of raucous sound. This was no everyday attack, of the kind she was used to, this was an astonishing power launched at her in vengeful fury, which swelled to proportions beyond belief.

Cringing painfully, she felt sharp invisible claws rake down her back and arms. The pins flew from her hair, releasing it to be whipped around her face, by a hot wind that rose from the floor thrashing the strands painfully across her cheeks.

She moaned in terror, utterly powerless to do anything but submit to the onslaught and pray that it soon pass.

The electric light flickered on and off at breathtaking speed, until with a loud crash the bulb exploded, sending shards of hot glass raining around the room, some embedding itself into the wall itself.

Crouching on the floor with her arms above her head in an effort to shield herself Jan prayed as she had never prayed before, for surely the Devil himself had been unleashed.

Something or someone was calling her over and over again. She lowered her arms, the room was quiet, untouched, walls, window, light fitting all undamaged. The water in the bath was sending spirals of fragrant steam into the air. This voice though was one she did recognise for on the other for on the other side of the door her little boy was calling her.

Totally worn down with exhaustion and constant spiritual attack, Jan struggled to make the day as normal for the children as was humanly possible. Inwardly she was utterly defeated, no one believed her, no one ever saw or heard any of the dreadful things she was forced to suffer day after day. It seemed that she was totally unable to escape the forces that had unleashed themselves against her. What could they want from her?

She made a pot of coffee and pouring a cup, forced herself to drink it. It tasted alien to her, bitter and burnt; yet she knew it was neither. Her stomach revolted as the warm liquid reached it and with a heave she lurched to the sink and brought it back up.

When he came home, David was amazingly calm when Jan asked him where he had been the night before.

"Didn't you realise how worried I would be?" she stormed at him, "David, how could you, in view of all that I am having to put up with at the moment?"

"Oh not that again Jan," he said firmly, "I naturally assumed you would realise that I had been called away."

"Why would I?" Jan was shedding angry tears, "It's not something you make a habit of and in any case there was a time when you wouldn't have dreamt of doing such a thing without letting me know somehow."

"Well times are different now, aren't they?" David said coldly. "Anyway, how exactly, could I have let you know, any suggestions? We don't have the telephone connected yet remember."

"Surely you could have driven home first and told me, anything to save me worrying."

"Jan you worry about everything," he said sarcastically, "Whatever I had chosen to do would have elicited some sort of complaint from you."

She couldn't believe he was being so cold and unfeeling. '

Later that evening, over a meal of cottage pie, David and she spoke little to each other, both pretending deep concentration upon the food before them. The ticking of the kitchen clock, exaggerated in the heavy silence, irritated Jan beyond belief.

David had noticed the coils of wire and handsets when he came in but had said nothing, merely giving them a cursory glance. Jan couldn't be bothered to explain why the phone was not yet connected, if he couldn't be bothered to ask. One small measure of how far they had grown apart.

Finishing his meal, David drained his wine glass then standing, pushed the chair back noisily on the floor.

"I'm going for a shower," he said curtly and left the room.

Jan sat dejectedly pushing the food on her plate around with the fork, laying it down she pushed the plate away from her. She wondered, yet again, why it was, that although she was in such great trouble, she couldn't discuss it with David. She missed the husband he had been, one that she could have confided in about anything, knowing he would have patiently listened, calmed and supported her. More than anything, she wanted this evil that had changed him and was wrecking their marriage, destroyed, yet its very malevolence it seemed, was preventing that from taking place. Lowering her head she began to sob as though her heart would break.

David was a long time taking his shower; Jan knew that he was deliberately keeping out of her way. Eventually he came down and took him himself into the drawing room switching on the television. She supposed the best way to get through this was to act as if nothing had happened, she would join him in the drawing room and hopefully, the volatile atmosphere would eventually ease, but first she must check upon the children.

After passing through the 'cold spot' a subtle shift in the air around her warned her that something was about to happen, the whispers began taunting her once again and sure enough as she reached the landing another manifestation was taking place, this time it was a man.

As the spectre took on clearer features Jan gasped for they were chilling indeed. Evil dark eyes that she felt looked into her very soul, blazed from his angular face whilst the lips of the apparition were pressed tightly together almost in a contemptuous sneer. She recoiled feeling the rails at the side of the staircase pressing into her back. She found she was unable to take her eyes off him although to remain doing so filled her with terror.

She toyed with the idea of calling David but if the apparition were to vanish before he saw it, he would once again be angry, accusing her of imagining the whole thing or at the worst having made it up.

The man began to move towards her, terrified Jan shrank back and tried to move backwards down the stairs. She misjudged the edge of the stair she aimed for, lost her footing and tumbled backwards reaching out for the rail to save her but missing. Just like a rag doll tossed a great height she felt the full length of the great staircase.

At the sound of her cries, David came rushing out of the drawing room to find her in a crumpled heap at the foot of the stairs.

Miraculously she wasn't badly hurt, badly shocked and with bruises already appearing on her arms and legs she appeared to have suffered no serious injury. This established, far from sympathising with the accident, David berated her clumsiness blaming the heels on the shoes she wore for causing the accident. She knew better than to tell him what had really taken place.

For a few days he was almost kind to her, apart from constantly complaining that her carelessness had necessitated him having to take absence from work he could ill afford, Daily he went on about how much his work load would be increasing, putting pressure on others of his team, whilst he was out of the office at home taking care of her. However he attended to her needs and those of the children, for which she found herself pathetically grateful.

On the evening of the third day following her fall, Jan went up to bed early with a severe headache. She turned back the bedspread and switched on the bedside lamps, which cast a soft apricot glow over the predominantly cream room.

Crossing to the window to close the curtains, she looked out pressing her face and aching forehead, close to the cold glass. Snow was still falling, thicker than ever; it had already coated the balcony with a fresh layer. The wind was whistling eerily through the eaves, having risen in the last hour, heralding another wild night. She closed the curtains on the chilly scene and as she was getting undressed, without any warning, the blood-curdling cry of terror of a young child rent the air, cutting the silence like a swathe through water.

Her immediate thought being that there was something wrong with one of her children, Jan fled from the room to check on them, but found both sleeping peacefully. Leaving their rooms, she edged back into the corridor fearful of what had caused the sound she had heard, she waited for it to come again but the only sound was that of the whispering which once again surrounded her as she struggled to slow her frantically beating heart. The cry rose again, ebbed then died away.

Jan stood rooted the spot, still trembling although now, all was quiet. She heard David walking up the stairs and waited for him to walk the length of the corridor to find her. After several moments he had still not appeared. She had heard no door open so knew he had not entered any of the rooms so where had he gone? She certainly hadn't heard him go back down stairs again. Needing to find him, she returned downstairs herself only to find that he was fast asleep on the sofa, with the television still turned on. Once again her heart speeded up as she felt the now familiar fear kicking in, for if David had been down here all the time, then who had it been, that she had heard walk up the stairs?

Deciding to leave him where he was, at least for the time being, Jan returned to bed although she was far too disturbed to sleep. She picked up her book and attempted to lose herself in the light-hearted novel but found herself reading the same piece over and over again. It had been a difficult book to get into in any event, due to the huge amount of characters the story contained. Each time someone was mentioned, Jan found she had to turn back several pages to discover who they were and where they fitted into the scheme of things. She wondered what made a writer do that, they surely couldn't realise what hard work it made reading the story. This book was even more complex due to the fact that at least half a dozen of the characters names began with the same letter. These things apart, her concentration was poor anyway, her mind always drifting back to thoughts of the house and its uninvited guests. She knew that there were now at least two spirits in the house, a man and a woman and there were children as well, having heard if not seen them. Every few minutes she found her eyes darting around the room or that subconsciously, she was holding her breath listening for anything out of the ordinary. What an appalling way to live, she thought, without suffering from agoraphobia for the situation was such that she was now not only afraid to be in the house no matter what evil it held, but also terrified of leaving it.

Time ticked on and still David had not come to bed, so Jan decide to go down and wake him, she was thirsty and needed to get a drink a water anyway.

Nervously, her eyes darting everywhere, she crossed the landing and made her way carefully down the stairs, her knee which had been the most badly bruised during her fall was still very stiff making walking extremely painful, down stairs particularly so.

David had moved from the sofa and was sitting in the chair with his back to the door. There were no lamps on, the only light in the room given off from the dying embers of the fire. As he didn't turn around at her entrance, she assumed he had dozed off again. However just as she was about to leave the room he turned around and fixed his gaze upon her.

Jan expected him to ask why she had come down, but he said nothing, in fact he was looking at her as though she were not even there.

Confused at his strange behaviour Jan cleared her throat and asked if he would like a drink, as she was about to make one. It was then that the strangest thing happened. David's appearance began to undergo a weird alteration, the shape and contour of his face changing dramatically. To her horror she saw that superimposed over her husband's features were those of the man who had materialised at the top of the stairs, causing her to fall.

Aghast Jan backed away slowly, not stopping until her back hit the door frame, and then jolted into action she turned wrenched open the door and fled back upstairs.

Not knowing what else to do, she got back into bed, sitting with her arms clasped around her knees, as she struggled to come to terms with the significance of what she had seen. Could it mean that her husband was being taken over by the male spirit in Challoners? Did such a thing really happen outside of films such as The Exorcist, she wondered? The truth of the matter was she didn't know what to think. If indeed possession was possible, it would she supposed be one explanation for the dramatic change in David's personality of late. Although she tried to rationalise her wildly racing imagination, living in this house and having experienced so many unbelievable things, she was now ready to be convinced that anything was possible.

Her main concern was how she was supposed to react when and if David eventually came up to bed, how did she know whether he really was her husband and if he wasn't then where had David gone? Round and round in her head went a myriad of questions she couldn't begin to find an answer to.

She lay down and shivered beneath the covers as at last she heard the sound she had been dreading, footsteps climbing the stairs. She braced herself not knowing just who would be coming through the door.

"Good, you're still awake; I've brought you a cup of tea."

Speechless she sat up and took the offered cup from her husband who smiled fondly at her.

"Th. Thank you," she stuttered, I was thirsty."

"Why didn't you come and tell me, I would have made you one earlier," he replied.

Jan watched him closely, realising that he had absolutely no idea that she had been downstairs and witnessed the odd transformation in the drawing room, if indeed he himself had been aware of what was happening to him and she doubted that he did. Or yet again, there was always the possibility that it was another of the tricks that the spirits in this infernal house persisted in playing upon her.

CHAPTER 12

The Engineer finally returned the next day in the midst of chaos, Paul having fallen down the stairs earlier. He wasn't really hurt just shaken and extremely irritable. The baby sensing his disquiet wouldn't stop crying either and Jan being thoroughly overtired, her nerves already in shreds, was finding it difficult to cope.

As she had come down the stairs that morning, shadows of something with no solid form, had appeared on the wall beside her and moved as if keeping up with her, accompanying the whispering she now expected to hear. Words that were impossible to make out and yet which, she felt were important if she could only hear. It had been then that Paul, who was following her, had tripped and fallen.

Later when he had recovered from his initial shock, he had asked to be allowed to go outside and play. Jan had refused, resulting in Paul throwing one of his rare tantrums. With both children screaming at the top of their voices, she was feeling acutely embarrassed as she answered the front door to let engineer in.

"My word you're having a fine old time of it today," he declared sympathetically.

Jan nodded, "they're not usually like this." It's been one of those days I'm afraid."

Paul looked at the engineer and stopped screaming immediately, smiling shyly, his face behind his hands, miraculously Sarah stopped crying as well.

"If that's the effect you have on my children, "Jan said with relief, "You are welcome here at any time."

"Got four kids of my own, comes with practice," the engineer replied and collecting the cable and handsets from beneath the hall table, he set off upstairs whistling, with Paul trotting after him.

"Come down here Paul, please."

"It's okay, let him come if he wants to. He won't be in the way. You can help me, can't you son?"

Paul gave Jan a smug 'I told you so' look and scurried up after the man importantly.

Sarah had begun crawling a couple of days earlier, so Jan had to keep her in the playpen now all the time, unless in the same room with her.

She couldn't believe how different the atmosphere felt with the engineer around. She could hear him whistling as he worked, in between chatting to Paul, whom she could just make out over the whispering which had now dropped to a low level, was earnestly explaining all about the bridge he was building for his train set.

All too soon, the engineer had finished and was sitting in the kitchen with her having a cup of tea. She had offered one, needing to hold on to a few more minutes of his comforting presence in the house.

"There shouldn't be any problems," he said, "But in the unlikely event that there is, get your husband to give this number a ring," and he handed her a small white card.

"Desperate to keep him there a little longer, Jan tried to make conversation and asked if he had lived in the village for long.

"All my life," he said, "sad isn't it? Of course I have thought about moving several times, but well, the wife likes it here, all her family are close and we're used to it I suppose. It really is pretty most of the year. You just wait and see, when the weather improves you won't know the place."

"I suppose you don't know anything of the history of this house do you?" she asked hopefully.

He shook his head," Not really, other than that it has been empty for about two years and before that, I believe it was used as Offices for a while, by the council, whilst they were waiting for their new building to be finished. The library at Milborough may have some information though if you're interested, they have a well stocked reference section there I believe, I don't read much myself but the wife does." He stood up and took his cup and saucer to the sink, "thanks for the tea, better be getting on, I've a full day ahead as usual," he grinned ruefully.

Jan saw him to the door, remaining on the porch until his van had disappeared from sight. Returning inside, yawning loneliness engulfed her once again. She decided that now the phone was connected she would ring Kate and attempt to mend bridges. There was an aching loneliness inside her for the loss of their friendship.

Dialling the familiar number, Jan felt her mouth drying with nervousness, for she had no idea how Kate would respond to her call. When there was no reply other than the robotic answer-phone message, she didn't know whether to be disappointed or relieved.

Paul ran upstairs to his train set and to get on with building his bridge. Jan was not to come into the room until it was finished he'd told her firmly.

Unable to apply herself to the painting or even housework, Jan played with Sarah for a while, and read her a story, pointing out the colourful pictures to the baby. Sarah had not slept well the previous night, she was cutting a tooth again and one side of her face was hotly inflamed. Before the story was finished, the baby had slumped forward in the playpen and fallen asleep.

Jan closed the book and left the chair beside the playpen. She had a pile of washing to be done and went to load the machine, whilst the baby was quiet. As she reached the doorway of the Utility room, a strong smell hit her, overpoweringly nauseating, a smell of decay and decomposing material, something old, hiding amongst the shadows. She clapped her hand over her mouth and nose, wherever could it be coming from, a blocked drain perhaps?

She hurried inside the room, but the sink there was as bright and shining white as she had left it, no sign of a clogged drain. The kitchen similarly so, then as suddenly as she had become aware of it, the smell completely disappeared.

Hearing a scratching at the back door, Jan ignore it believing it to be yet another of the tricks the house played on her, it went on and on until, she had to know what was outside causing the sound. Plucking up courage she opened it a crack, there to her utmost relief, cold wet and bedraggled but very much alive, was the cat.

For once deeply asleep, Jan was dreaming. In her idyllic dream world, she was lying on a soft, sandy beach bathed in warm sunshine. Surf lapped gently on the shore and a faint warm breeze stirred her hair. Blissfully relaxed, she luxuriated in the dream, irritated that the crying of a baby disturbed it. Turning on her stomach and burying her head in the pillow, she tried to shut out the invasive sound, but it would not be shut out. The crying became more and more distressed, alarmed she woke with a start – Sarah?

She leapt out of bed, reaching that instant state of wakefulness that only mothers with young children, seem able to do within minutes of rousing. Running barefoot along the corridor to Sarah's room, she found the baby fast asleep, lying on her stomach, snuffling slightly into the mattress, but she realised she could still hear a baby crying.

Room by room, shutting out her fear of the house at night, she searched for the source of the sound. She had the weirdest sensation as if her thoughts were divided, she knew of course that she had her own children, yet something compelled her to look for two other children that she somehow knew should be in the house also.

David met her in the corridor shuffling half asleep out of their room.

"Jan, what on earth are you doing wandering around the house at night?"

"The baby," she cried, "I have to find the baby."

"What do you mean has Sarah gone?" David was instantly wide awake, and looking at her with undisguised horror.

"No not Sarah, the other baby."

"What other baby?"

"David, are you deaf?" she shrieked at him, her eyes blazing. "There, can you hear it?"

To placate her David obediently listened, too tired to argue at length, the house was totally silent.

"See," said Jan, "I have to find it. Help me David please," she implored, taking hold of his arm and tugging, her eyes beseeching.

He shook her, "Jan there is no other baby in this house, there is no-one crying, there isn't a sound, and it must have been a dream nothing more."

"There is, there is, I can still hear it, Oh God I must find it, it needs help."

"David lost his temper banging his fist on the occasional table nearby. "Stop it Jan, there is no baby crying! "

Then, "Sssh," she whispered, "It's stopped, oh David thank goodness it's stopped."

Somehow David coaxed her back to bed, but she found it impossible to get back to sleep and lying fully awake, sheer despair washed over her. Why, whatever evil entity was in this house was affecting her alone, she had no idea, or she was indeed losing her mind? She found herself hyperventilating, nauseous and totally helpless, for fear stalked her every waking moment. Why her, she wondered what had she ever done to deserve this? Did there linger here some bitter spirit who having lost her own children was punishing Jan because her children were still alive?

Jan had thought that things couldn't get a lot worse, yet when David returned from work the following day with the news that his firm were sending to Scotland for two weeks where they were opening up a new laboratory, she was speechless with fear.

"I've had an idea," he said quickly noting the panic in her eyes, he'd expected "ask your parents to come and stay, why not give them a ring now? I am sure they'd welcome the chance for a few days break even in this weather."

Jan went into the hall and sat on the curved stone seat they bought at a garden sale, before they had moved into the house and dialled her parent's number, she found herself experiencing a thrill merely from being able to pick up the telephone and ring someone.

"Mum. Mum is that you?" The line was faint. "You sound so far away."

"Yes, I can hear you perfectly," was the reply," no need to shout darling, are you all well?"

Jan swallowed, over the weeks since they had lived in Challoners, she would have dearly loved to be able to confide in her parents, but knew already what their reaction would be. At first startled, then amazed, distressed and fearful of things they knew nothing of and even less understood and she had decided she could not burden them with her problems.

They chatted for a few minutes, before Jan told them of David's trip and asked if they would like to come to stay, to keep her and the children company.

"Of course we'd love to, it will be lovely to spend a fortnight with the little ones I miss them so much, when is David leaving?"

Jan realised he hadn't told her, "Hang on Mum I'll go and ask".

She lay the receiver down and called to David who was playing on the floor with the children tickling them, both were giggling hysterically.

"What day are you leaving?"

"Oh yeah, sorry I forgot to say, tomorrow straight after work."

"Tomorrow? Nice of them to give us so much warning," she replied sarcastically, "I had no idea it would be that soon".

David made a wry face and for a second looked marginally uncomfortable, then turned his attention back to his children.

Jan picked up the receiver again. "Hello Mum, Mum?" but there was no reply for the line was quite dead.

****

David and she took turns throughout the evening to try ringing again, but all their efforts proved futile, for they were unable to even obtain as much as a dialling tone. Abandoning it for the time being, they tried again next morning, but to their frustration, the telephone was still out of order.

Jan gave David the card the engineer had left with her and he promised to call as soon as he reached the office. "I'll phone your Mum and Dad as well," he reassured her. "They've already said they'll come, so you have no need to worry that you are going to be left on your own."

He picked up the suitcase he'd packed the previous evening, gave her a half hearted kiss upon the cheek and hugging both of the children, he left.

After he had gone, Jan tried to occupy her herself with odd jobs around the house. She was desperate for the telephone to be fixed, feeling very vulnerable now David had left and would not be returning for two weeks.

Gathering the paint and brushes together, she intended to repaint the woodwork in the small bedroom, which was to be Sarah's new nursery. For the time being Sarah had been sleeping in a room next to Paul, as David had insisted she be moved out of their bedroom.

David had moved out all the furniture from the old nursery, with the exception of the mobile, which he had been instructed to throw away. He had put it into the dustbin and the first time Jan had gone out to put rubbish inside, she had seen the swans, which set her trembling so she had shoved them quickly down the bottom, out of sight beneath the rubbish.

She was almost through painting the windowsill a delicate shade of creamy pink, and ignoring the persistent whispering which had begun again as soon as she had entered the room, when the telephone rang.

Excitedly realising the fault must now be fixed, she leapt to answer. It was David.

"That was quick," she replied, "getting the fault sorted out I mean."

"Yes odd that, they checked the line and said there wasn't anything wrong with it and told me to try calling you and well, it's fine again now so it must have been the weather or something."

"Yes, or something," she muttered, too quietly for him to hear.

"I've rung your parents," David continued, "and they'll be arriving about 7.30 ish. They are catching a coach at midday and will get a cab from Milborough to Challoners. They're thrilled at the prospect of seeing you all again"

"That will cost them a small fortune," Jan said worriedly.

"No it won't I've rung the cab company and told them to put it on my credit card."

"Oh thanks David that was thoughtful of you." Jan was quite surprised at his thoughtfulness in view of how uncaring he had seemed of late.

"Well they are doing me a favour by staying with you."

Jan was excited and relieved that the preparations had been made for her parents' visit. She didn't think she could have borne a fortnight in the house with just the children for company.

"There's so much to do," she babbled, "making up the beds and cooking and I'll have to shelve the painting for the time being."

"Plenty of time for that, now don't worry, I'll phone as often as I can, and with your parents there the time will fly," he assured her. "Tell Paul I'll bring him something nice back."

Jan giggled, "He wants a haggis. He thinks it's an animal which he can keep as a pet."

David's laughter filled her ears, she revelled in the sound, how long she wondered, had it been since she had heard him genuinely laugh like that? Saying goodbye and she loved him, she reluctantly replaced the receiver.

She returned light heartedly, to the little bedroom to collect the paint and brushes. The scene that met her gaze as she opened the door made her gasp aloud. White paint had been splashed all over the pale pink walls, thick and congealing, it ran down in rivulets gathering in little sticky puddles on the newly laid, rose pink carpet. Crawling amidst the paint, were a cloud of black flies, which buzzed angrily as the paint stuck to their wings. The window was wide open, through which no doubt the flies had found had found their way inside.

Convinced that Paul must be responsible, Jan called him.

"Paul, come here at once."

He came trotting up the stairs humming a tuneless little song, trailing his tattered old teddy bear behind him.

"Jan snapped. "Whatever have you done you naughty boy?" Grabbing hold of his shoulder, she dragged him through the door to survey the mess. "You know you are not allowed to touch paint, whatever were you thinking of? As for opening the window, Paul I've lost count of how many times I've told you never to go near windows or open them, you know how dangerous it could be? As it is, it has let all these nasty flies in."

"I don't know what you mean Mummy, I didn't do anything," Paul sobbed, "I didn't open the window and there aren't any flies anyway."

Jan wrenched her gaze from him and back into the room, there was no spilt paint, no open window and of the flies there was no sign, the room was exactly as she had left it before answering the telephone.

CHAPTER 13

The afternoon light began to fade and toward dusk, the fog swept in. From the distant hills it rolled across the snow covered meadow and lawns surrounding the house and settled, enveloping the house in a thick white freezing shroud. Snow and fog thought Jan grimly, looking out of the window, could anything be worse, she could barely see where the lawn began, visibility ending at the edge of the patio.

The children were fractious, Sarah, still teething was inconsolable, finally Jan gave her a dose of calpol, which soothed her, and she fell asleep. Jan carried her carefully up the stairs and put her in her cot. Paul, first upset by his Mothers outbreak, then filled with excitement at the prospect of seeing his Nan and Granddad, had begun fooling around and tumbled over grabbing as he fell an occasional table on which was one of Jan's cherished possessions which smashed the moment it hit the floor. It was a large Murano glass vase that David had bought for her as a souvenir on the Rialto Bridge in Venice, during their honeymoon.

Jan was furious, she sent Paul to bed early, telling him that he would not be allowed to sit up and see his Grandparents, but would have to wait until the morning. On hands and knees, she swept up the rainbow coloured glass fragments. She knew she shouldn't have been so harsh with him, it was really her own fault if it was anybody's, she should have known better than to have placed it on a low table with a small child in the house. The vase should have been kept in a high place; better still in one of her cabinets, but it had looked so beautiful on the small table in the window bay, the light shining through the coloured glass. She sat back on her heels, fighting down the impulse to bring her son downstairs again. To her surprise she found tears trickling down her cheeks as she remembered back to those halcyon days, when the vase had been bought.

Following a fairytale white wedding, their honeymoon had been the stuff dreams are made of, a fortnight in Venice, their life together stretching before them full of promise. She fought down a lump in her throat as she compared those happy times with what they were living through now.

The hotel David had chosen for them had been fearfully expensive. She had protested with the argument that it was a great deal of money to spend on accommodation and that surely there had been somewhere cheaper they could have stayed.

"Rubbish," David had said, "We only get one honeymoon, and it is going to be special."

Jan had never before stayed anywhere so luxurious and was quite overwhelmed by its quiet splendour.

After dinner on their first evening, they had wandered out in to the sultry heat to explore, crossing a small white stone bridge they had stood looking down into the canal beneath them.

A Gondolier had gestured to them to come and take a ride and they had done so, gliding along the Grand Canal in the encroaching dusk, beneath the many bridges each one differently designed.

It had been all the more special simply because it was Jan's first ever trip abroad let alone their honeymoon. It proved to be a fascinating voyage of discovery as the ancient city revealed itself to them layer by colourful layer.

Sunset tingeing the canal water a dull rusty red, they glided on, past the age worn exteriors of stone buildings, ablaze with colour from window boxes full of flowers.

Later, on leaving the gondola, they had wandered the streets; some so narrow they could only be negotiated by walking in single file. A bell sounded loud and clear and rounding a corner they'd found themselves knee deep in pigeons in St Mark's Square. People teemed around them, Jan had clasped David's arm tightly afraid they'd become separated in the crowd. He had made her feel so safe, so protected; she would give anything she thought to feel like that again.

Walking back to their hotel, they had crossed the Rialto Bridge and it had been then, that the fantastic array of glass displayed in the windows had caught their eyes. Glass, which was produced on the tiny island of Murano, just a water- bus ride away.

The glass was truly fascinating, in all colours of the rainbow, many shot through with real gold and silver. The shapes of the bowls and vases waved in drippy curved lines utterly unique. David wanted to buy her a piece and wandering into the small store, Jan had seen instantly the vase she knew she would like to own. It was quite large and was the most gorgeous aqua blue-green, shot though with deeper shades of emerald and royal blue. A dusting of pure silver scattered throughout completed its magical appearance, somehow it reminded her of the ocean. It was wrapped, paid for and carried carefully back to England, and had remained with her until now, when it lay in rainbow shards upon the floor.

She swept it up and wrapping it carefully in newspaper dropped it in the kitchen bin and got on with making a Chicken Chasseur, her parents' favourite meal.

For once no snow was falling but eerie wisps of fog blew past the window in the rising wind. Night was closing in, another few hours and her parents would arrive, how she looked forward to seeing them again.

She set the cooker timer, placing the prepared dish inside the oven and whipped cream for the pudding, having already defrosted the raspberries, which she had chosen to follow the first course.

As it was a special occasion, Jan decided it would be nice to eat in the dining room, David, she and the children usually ate in the kitchen. She opened drawers selecting napkins, place mats and cutlery with which to lay the table. She took a bottle of wine out of the rack and placed it in the fridge to cool, remembering also to collect her best crystal wine glasses from the cabinet in the drawing room.

Just as she had finished setting the table and was standing back admiring how pretty it looked, the telephone rang, thinking it was probably David, she hurried to answer it.

"Hullo?"

"Oh Jan it's Mum."

"Mum, where are you, you haven't been delayed have you? I thought by now you would have been on the coach."

"It's your Dad," a sob broke into her Mother's voice, "Oh Jan darling, I'm afraid he's had a heart attack. It happened at the coach station as we were waiting for the bus, he suddenly felt poorly and had a really bad pain in his chest and arm. People have been ever so kind, ringing the doctor and everything for us. There was no time to call before, what with the ambulance arriving and everything. Anyway we're at the hospital now and he's been examined.

"Oh Mum how dreadful, is he going to be alright?"

"We think so, they've managed to stabilise him, but he's in intensive care and they tell me that the next forty- eight hours are critical. I must stay with him of course. I'm so sorry dear to let you down. Who would have thought such a thing would happen?"

"Mum don't worry about any of that, the main thing is that Dad is okay."

"All right dear, well I'd better be getting back to him, I told him I'd just be a little while ringing you. I'll ring again if there's any change otherwise I'll ring tomor..." static prevented her from hearing her mothers last words, which grew louder and louder. Then there was an abrupt silence as the static ceased, almost as if it were gaining strength, before bombarding her hearing with yet more harsh crackles and hissing. She held the receiver away from her ear, afraid to listen, yet afraid to put the receiver down. When at last she forced herself to listen again, the line was quite dead once again.

Jan sat down heavily upon the hall seat, replacing the receiver. Her poor, poor Dad, thank God he was alive. Then the realisation of what the news meant to her, for she was now faced with spending two weeks in Challoners alone, whether she liked it or not.

* * * *

She decided it would be a good idea to try to have an early night. Her mother's news had drained what little mental energy she had left, so heavy hearted, she turned off the oven, unable to face eating anything of the meal she'd prepared, it would have to do for tomorrow. Putting everything away again would give her one more job to carry out to help pass the time tomorrow.

She followed her usual nightly routine of closing all the doors downstairs and turning off the lights. Passing through the hall on her way up the stairs, the dead telephone mocked her from the hall table.

She went into the bathroom, turned on the light and filled the basin with warm water. After splashing her face she patted it dry catching sight of her reflection in the mirror, which hung above the basin. She found herself wondering not for the first time, why the glass never looked really clean, always appearing to be covered with a greasy film, no matter how much she polished it. It wasn't, she noticed with a start looking like that now however, for once it was crystal clear and with a shock she realised that the image that looked back at her was not her own. She blinked but the image remained, it was the image of the woman she had seen several times now, with the sad expression in the far too pale face.

Jan whipped around believing the woman must be standing behind her to be so reflected in the mirror but save for her, the room was quite empty. Returning her gaze to the image, she saw it was fading, her own reflection being now superimposed over that of the woman. In seconds she could see her no longer.

As she made her way to bed, Jan attempted to rationalise what she had seen, after all a mirror was simply a sheet of silvered glass, it couldn't contain anything, surely the image must have been formed by her mind's subconscious this time? It was yet another question that would remain unanswered.

The telephone rang several times the next morning and each time Jan hurried toward it anxiously expecting it to be David, or her mother with eagerly awaited news of her Dad's condition. Each time she had picked up the receiver, she had heard the familiar whispering, she was so used to hearing around the house, or static so loud, she'd had no alternative but to hang up.

After a brief half hour of silence, the telephone rang again. Paul entered the hall, where Jan was leaning against the kitchen doorframe looking at the telephone with loathing.

"Aren't you going to answer it Mummy? O.K. I will," and before she could stop him Paul had bounded across the hall and picked up the receiver.

"Hullo, who's calling?" he asked importantly, then "Oh hello daddy, yes she's here."

Almost choking with relief, Jan leapt across the hall and seized the receiver Paul held out to her.

Their conversation consisted mainly, of Jan relaying to David the devastating news she had received from her Mother the night before. By the time she hung up, she was even more depressed because sympathetic as he had been, David had not once mentioned how she was coping, faced with being alone in the house but for the children and she for her part had not dared suggest that he might be able to cut short his stay in Scotland due to the circumstances.

* * * *

Evening fell; Jan sat in the drawing room half heartedly watching the television. She had flicked through all the channels, but had found nothing, which really interested her. Party because she had so much on her mind. The room was reasonably warm but she found she was shivering.

Suddenly, footsteps sounded above her, not the quick footsteps she had heard before but slow lagging steps, heavy, as if each foot was being slowly but firmly placed one before the other. The room was becoming colder and Jan was seized with a fresh fit of shivering which caused her teeth to chatter. Afraid to move, she sat cloaked in breathless expectancy, but for the moment at least there were no more disturbances, the footsteps died away and she could no longer hear them.

Her Mother had rung earlier, for once and surprisingly; the whole conversation had taken place without the familiar static cutting in or the line going dead. The news had been neither good nor bad. Her Dad was still in intensive care but remaining stable with little change in his condition. Jan had been relieved to hear from her Mother as the concern she had about her dad was putting an even greater strain on her mind, which was already dangerously close to breaking point.

She felt a vague irritation on her arm and rubbed at it absently, feeling her fingers wet, she glanced at her arm and was astonished to see that it was spattered with bright red blood. Rubbing it away, she was surprised to see that there was no wound, so she had not scratched herself without realising. Two more drops appeared and something drew her gaze upward. To her utter horror, blood was steadily dripping from the ceiling. Horrified, she leapt out of her chair and bolted up the stairs two at a time in her anxiety to reach the room above, which she had worked out, was Sarah's old nursery

Heart thudding painfully, she wrenched back the bolt and threw open the door, half afraid that this time she would actually see something her mind would not be able to stand up to, but she found nothing, the room was as still and quiet as it should be. When she returned to the drawing room, no sign of the blood remained, but what she found instead, frightened her even more.

A pattern of extraordinary complexity had been made on the floor from the myriad of coloured yarns trailing from her sewing box, which stood open on the rug before the fire.

For a few seconds Jan looked at it utterly fascinated, it would have taken any human being hours to contrive such a pattern, yet she had been out of the room five minutes at the utmost. With a strangled sob, she dropped to her knees and frenziedly scraped up the yarns and threw the whole tangled heap into the fire. At once there was a vigorous pounding on the ceiling, whilst glancing behind her, she had a tantalising glimpse of something crossing her vision, something she had narrowly missed seeing.

Over the next days, more and more strange things began to happen. Strange meaningless things such as a book pulled out of a neatly aligned row on the bookcase, impossibly balanced in the air, only one third of it left actually remaining on the shelf. Jan had pushed it back with one finger, recoiling as she felt it cold as a block of ice and resisting her touch.

At other times loud banging on the ceiling or walls would startle her, sounds that loud as they were, never disturbed her children, it seemed they were totally out of their hearing. Jan was mortally afraid, for her instincts warned her that things were building toward a crescendo. Many of the things were such as could have been carried out by a mischievous child, with items like the children's slippers being found in the refrigerator. Such things in any other circumstances would have made Jan laugh, but not any more.

On the fourth day of David's absence, Jan stood at the sink carefully watering her violets on the window-sill. Feeling an extremely cold draught sweep across her legs, she left the watering to seek the cause and found the front door wide open, gusts of cold air were blowing inside carrying with them fine flakes of snow, the weather having worsened yet again.

"Paul," she called anxiously.

"I'm here Mummy," he poked his head around the drawing room door.

"Did you open this door?"

"No Mummy, I can't reach the handle."

Jan realised that it was true, there was no way Paul could have reached it without standing on something, which obviously had not been the case.

She knew that no one could have got in from outside without a key, so felt compelled to search the house. Finding nothing downstairs, she hurried to the next floor. Halfway up the stairs she hit another icy cold spot, an indication she had grown used to of something unearthly about to happen. Making her way nervously to the top and through the second cold spot, she was horrified to see a black shape forming outside the old nursery door, taking on the shape of the woman, Jan had now seen on several occasions. This time it was different in as much as it was accompanied by a feeling of great anger, which Jan felt so strongly, she recoiled holding her head in her hands. The manifestation was different this time in that the figure was floating some six inches above the ground.

Jan jumped as a loud splintering crack rent the air. Turning, she saw that unbelievably, the window behind her had cracked from corner to corner. Then the next window along shattered sending icicles of glass hurtling through the air, from which she had to shield her eyes. The icy wind having found its way in, whipped the curtains chaotically.

One by one, each window along the landing cracked or shattered simultaneously.

Jan backed nervously down the stairs, holding tight to the rail, aware of the danger of falling once again, her feet crunching broken glass beneath her feet. Not for one moment did she take her face from the figure on the landing, which even as she watched shrank in upon itself and disappeared.

Reaching the bottom, trembling for each new apparition served only to make her nerves worse, she never got used to the things she saw, she found both children happily watching the children's cartoon show; as usual neither had heard anything.

As the credits began to roll across the television screen, indicating the end of the programme he had been watching, Paul jumped to his feet and announced he was going to play in his room and began running toward the stairs.

"No Paul, not now, the wind has broken a window, there's some broken glass on the stairs which I need to clear up first," her words trailed away for Paul had already reached the top of the stairs.

"Which window Mummy?" He called down to her, puzzled.

Jan swallowed and closed her eyes, for from his words, she knew already that if she were to go upstairs now, every window would be intact. Once again it would all have been an illusion. More tricks to wear her down to breaking point. No matter what evil force was causing these strange hallucinations; one thing was quite clear in Jan's mind, she had no hope of escaping them.

CHAPTER 14

Jan slept with the light on that night, although 'slept' was hardly the word, as she was afraid to close her eyes. All around her the atmosphere 'seethed' with impending disaster, she felt it gradually closing in threatening to suffocate her with its horror.

When the first grey fingers of dawn penetrated the curtains and she still had not slept a wink, she knew she could take no more, she had to seek help, but from where? Where did one go, with a problem of this nature and magnitude?

Wearily she dragged herself out of bed, her eyes gritty and sore, through lack of sleep. Days like this she knew that the children would be difficult sensing her extreme vulnerability and they would not be easy to handle. She was prepared for a difficult day ahead.

Toying with a cup of coffee she didn't really want, as the children ate their breakfast, Jan racked her brains over who would be the appropriate person to approach with her 'problem'. The church was the obvious answer, she supposed. Although not a regular churchgoer, Jan had been brought up to believe in God and it was fair to say her faith was unshakeable. She decided that she would look through the telephone directory in order to see if she could find the name of the church in Lesser Kirston. She waited until she had the children dressed and occupied with their toys, before carrying out her intentions.

Beneath the listing of Churches in the yellow pages, Jan found that Lesser Kirston's tiny little Norman church bore the impressive name of St Augustine of the Seven Martyrs, such a long name for the 'dolls house' of the Norman church she pondered idly. Beneath the name of the church, another listing gave Father Michael Stephens, as being the rector of the parish. She jotted the number down on the notepad beside the phone and closing the directory lifted the receiver to make the call, or attempt to, if the spirits in the house would let her; first ensuring Paul would not overhear her.

With shaking fingers Jan tapped out the number and heard it ring the other end, at first she thought no one was going to answer as it rang several times. A painful lump rose in her throat, as she realised how much she was pinning on this call. At last however, a soft, well educated voice announced, "Father Michael, how may I help?"

Jan swallowed, for she realised that she hadn't the first idea of where to start, to even broach such a subject.

"Hullo, Hullo, is anyone there?" the voice that was Father Michael repeated.

"Yes, yes hello, I'm sorry, I just don't really know where to begin." To her horror she found she was crying, tears sliding silently down her cheeks.

"That's quite all right my dear, take your time." Father Michael spoke kindly, sensing there was someone very troubled on the end of the line.

"My name is Jan. Father. Jan Blake. I, that is my husband and I and our two children, have recently moved into Lesser Kirston, a house called Challoners" she began.

"Ah yes, I know it, lovely old place, been empty for some time though I believe. I do apologise, I hadn't realised there was a family living there now, I would have paid a visit to welcome you to our parish."

"Well, you see it's like this," Jan went on falteringly, "there are some very strange things happening here in the house, but they only appear to be happening to me, my husband doesn't believe me, the children seem oblivious to what's going on and well." she broke off, unable to find the words to finish the sentence.

"I see, well don't try to explain any more just now if it is difficult for you, I wonder could you manage to come to the Vicarage and see me?"

"I don't have any transport I'm afraid, and anyway I don't actually drive."

"Ah, well then, in that case I will come to you." He coughed softly and cleared his throat, "I'll just fetch my diary and we'll make a date convenient to you, I think the sooner the better don't you?"

"Oh Thank you father, so much," Jan's relief was immeasurable; at long last someone was going to listen to her. She was clinging on to the receiver so hard, her knuckles whitened, as she waited for father Michael to return with his diary. Before he could do so however, the familiar static began on the line, Jan was neither deterred nor particularly surprised by it and when Father Michael picked up the receiver again she carried on speaking until it drowned her words completely, only then did she become really angry.

"Oh no you don't," she cried in frustration, "Whatever you are, you are not going to stop me."

But it was quite useless, all attempts at further conversation on the phone proved impossible as once the static died, the line had gone dead yet again. The pounding began on the ceiling and the chandelier swung wildly, its crystals drops tinkling.

Jan tried repeatedly to make another call to the Vicarage, her frustration growing as hour after hour passed and the line remained dead, her greatest fear being, that Father Michael may have thought she had ended the call voluntarily, thinking better of relaying her experiences.

Father Michael, however had no such thoughts, he replaced the receiver with a sinking feeling in his stomach and a deep frown wrinkling his placid features. He was no stranger to the static that had prevented the conversation from continuing. There was something alarming going on at Challoners, of that he had no doubt and was full of concern for the young woman and her family. He knew it would be futile attempting to ring her back, the same thing would only happen again, there was nothing for it he must go to her immediately.

Reluctantly but resolutely, leaving his comfortable chair by the fireside and the sermon he was writing for Sunday's service, he wandered into the kitchen to find his housekeeper, Mrs Matthews.

Father Michael had never married; it wasn't that his religion forbade it, but rather that after all his studying to enter the Church, there had never seemed to be the time to look for that special someone. Only in vague passing moments did he regret it, the Church more than filling his life with contentment. Lesser Kirston was a small Parrish but as any village, had its fair share of problems and there was little or no let up in the constant stream of parishioners to his door, seeking his help and support in times of need.

Mrs Matthews was standing at the sink peeling potatoes for the evening meal, which she would prepare before going home to attend to her own family. She had worked for Father Michael ever since he had moved to lesser Kirston three years previously. She bullied him in a motherly sort of way and they got on very well indeed.

Hearing him enter the room she turned and smiled.

"Anything I can get for you Father?"

"No, nothing at all Mrs Matthews thank you, I just came to tell you that I have to go out for a while to see a new parishioner."

"Oh dear and on such a nasty day as well."

Father Michael looked past his housekeeper's homely figure to the snow-covered garden visible from the window.

"It has turned into a very harsh winter indeed hasn't it? I look forward to being able to spend a few days in the garden again, when spring arrives." Gardening was a favourite hobby of Father Michael's, he was scarcely happier than when pottering in his greenhouse and took great pride from the fact that he raised most of his plants himself from seed.

"Wrap up warmly now won't you," fussed Mrs Matthews. "Do you have far to go?"

"No not too far, just outside the village."

Mrs Matthews wiped her hands and followed him to the hall, watching as he put on his overcoat, scarf and gloves. He took his car keys from the silver salver on the hall table and then went to fetch his Bible and prayer book, putting them into the battered old black leather briefcase that went everywhere with him. She was concerned to see that he also picked up and put into his case, a small bottle of Holy water, for she knew that meant he had dangerous things to attend to.

Mrs Matthews opened the front door for him, closing it quickly after he had stepped outside as the cold accompanied by a flurry of snowflakes rushed into the hall.

She couldn't help noticing that Father Michael had been wearing a worried expression and wondered what the problem might be, that had taken him away from a warm fireside and his sermon on such a hostile day. She never asked questions of him, it was not her business - her place was taking care of his house.

Father Michael hurried across the drive to the garage, his head bowed low to avoid the bitterly cold driving snow, which was stinging his cheeks. Unlocking the door he hurried to get into his car, anxious to get the car started and hoping the heater would warm up quickly. He had become frozen in just the short distance from the house, the bitter wind even finding its way through the thick overcoat he wore.

He drove off leaving dark tracks on the smooth white surface of the snow covered drive, waving to Mrs Matthews whom he could see watching his departure through the hall window. He gave a little smile, she always watched until she could see him no longer.

Turning the car into the lane he steered left towards the outskirts of lesser Kirston; his mind full of what he might discover when he reached Challoners.

* * * *

Jan was sitting on the floor of the drawing room with Paul playing Ludo. Sarah beside them in her playpen pulled herself to her feet by the bars watching fascinated, as they in turn moved their coloured counters around the board, glancing at her Jan thought it would be only a short time before the baby was walking.

"Come on Mummy, it's your turn."

"Sorry Paul, I wasn't concentrating."

Since the call made to Father Michael, Jan had clearly felt something in the atmosphere of the house change. It had always felt uncomfortable ever since the haunting had begun, but the air around her now appeared to be breathing hostility heavy with threatened foreboding.

'They're angry,' Jan thought 'They know I have decided to seek help and they don't like it.'

"Mummy. Mummy come on it's your turn again."

Jan turned her attention back to the game but sensing her reluctance Paul got to his feet, sweeping the counters off the board saying irritably, "I don't want to play any more anyway."

"I'm sorry Paul, it's just that, that," she struggled to think of a reason, "I've got a bad headache that's all."

Not answering Paul picked up his book of trains, announcing that he was going to play in his room. He stalked from the room defiantly.

Sighing heavily, Jan decided she must make an effort to involve herself in something which would distract her from how disturbingly afraid she was feeling. She couldn't think of a single thing so went to prepare the children's lunch. She hoped her Mother would ring soon, with news of her dad's progress. She picked up the receiver in the hall to see if the phone was working again yet and was reassured to hear the hum indicating that it was.

As she replaced the receiver, some instinct made her glance up the stairs. At the top a huge black form was gathering, of no particular shape, it seethed and wavered growing larger. Jan's first conscious thought was that it was between her and Paul, playing in his room and she was very frightened. The whispers surrounded her once again, louder than they had ever been before and heavy footsteps could be heard tramping back and forth above her somewhere. Jan bit her lip so hard she tasted blood, forced to watch horrified as the black mass began slowly rolling down the stairs towards her, behind it she was aware of a fleeting glimpse of someone, who looked suspiciously like Abigail Grinstead. Jan made to move but found she was unable to; she was helpless to do anything but watch as the mass slowly moved nearer threatening to envelope her.

It was halfway down the staircase when the doorbell rang jerking her from her frozen watchfulness. Finding herself able to move once again, she hurried to answer the door, at once the mass retreated and disappeared.

"Yes," she hissed, "You don't like being disturbed do you; you can't allow anyone else to see what you are doing to me." Her words were met by a thunderous knocking on the ceiling, which then seemed to come from the walls floor, everywhere. It stopped as soon as she opened the door.

Jan was immediately comforted to find that it was the Reverend on the doorstep. He had a kindly face, which mirrored sincerity and she immediately felt she could put her trust in him to help her. The long black robe he wore which was showing beneath his overcoat looked far too long and foolishly she found herself thinking it needed turning up an inch or so.

"You must be...?" she began.

"Yes, I'm Father Michael," he extended his hand and gripped hers in a warm firm clasp

"Do come inside, quickly Father out of the cold," Jan stood back as he entered as he did so, a powdering of snow falling from his shoulders to the hall floor.

Resting his briefcase on the floor, Father Michael removed his coat and hat and unwound his scarf; Jan took them and hung them in the cupboard.

"Do go in father," she indicated the drawing room, the door of which stood open. Little Sarah hauled herself to her feet hearing voices and strained her head in order to be able to take a look at the new arrival.

"I'm just about to put the baby down for her nap," Jan explained, "do please make yourself comfortable I won't be long.

Paul my little boy is playing in his room so we will be able to speak freely I don't want him to hear anything of what I have to tell you."

Smiling, she scooped up the baby and made to leave the room.

Father Michael watched her leave, her movements he felt were jerky and nervous, she looked far too thin and her face wore a careworn expression. He settled himself on the Chesterfield, one of the new pieces David had purchased and took in his surroundings, whilst he waited for Jan to return. It was a truly beautiful room with shades of a bygone elegant era. He had to admit he had been impressed with Challoners from the moment he had turned his car into the drive. Because it had been empty for long before he took over the parish he had never had cause to visit the house before and had often wondered what it was like, having passed its driveway many times on his travels.

Aware that the house was as quiet as death it was difficult for him to believe that two small lively children lived here. He was also very conscious that things were not as they should be. There was no doubt that Challoners had a thick, dark soupy atmosphere, which he had been uncomfortably aware of immediately he had stepped inside the front door, for it had enveloped him like a dank musty cloak. There were things in this house he knew he needed to deal with but hoped never to see.

In a short while, Jan had returned to the drawing room and sat on the edge of a chair facing him, her hands clasped tightly between her knees. His heart went out to her as he saw the stark fear in her eyes. She was he thought, a young woman who should not have known fear, gentle warm and loving wanting only to be happy and make a good home for her husband and children.

He smiled hoping to put her at her ease.

"How can I help?" he asked quietly, locking his fingers together in his lap.

She cleared her throat, "I don't know if anyone can help Father, I hardly know where to begin, so much has happened in such a short time you see and I am so dreadfully afraid."

"It's alright. Take your time. I'm here to listen and to help."

She made to get up, "Oh dear how rude of me. Could I get you a hot drink tea or coffee perhaps."

"Later," he gestured for her to remain seated, "when we have talked perhaps"

"You see, I've been hearing voices," she began, then catching herself hurriedly said, "Oh I know how that must sound, mentally disturbed people say that don't they?" she paused, "at least that's what David, my husband says," she paused, "I think the house is haunted father, I see things, hear noises, lights go on and off, things move around on their own and there is a dreadful cold spot at the top of the stairs, it's always there."

"Ah, lights noises, teleportation of objects all familiar and the classic 'cold' spot, typically associated with haunting, theorised to be caused by a drain on thermal energy, used by disembodied spirits to move objects or become visible. Go on." He moved forward a little in his seat.

For the next hour Jan related the events of the past weeks, her eyes, which only left his face now and again to dart nervously around the room, holding a world of despair.

Father Michael watched and listened carefully, she had gone quite pale, her hands trembling in her lap; there was little doubt in his mind that she was mortally afraid of what was happening to her.

Finishing speaking at last, Jan took a deep breath and closed her eyes. Opening them she waited to hear what he had to say in the wake of all she had related.

"You do believe me, don't you, Father?"

"I am certainly not here to make judgements, but yes I do believe you, I feel it myself, the evil in the house."

Father Michael rose to his feet and clasping his hands behind his back paced back and forwards across the rug as he spoke.

"Whatever the explanation for all these things, we must analyse them carefully. I think it would be a good idea for you to keep a diary of the events, every single detail that you can remember, could you do that?"

"Oh yes of course." Jan was anxious to agree.

"The clothing you described the phantom funeral party as wearing, sounded Victorian, and there were children's coffins, a great deal of children did not survive infancy in those days."

Jan leaned forward eagerly.

"Do you think that the house could be haunted by the people that lost the children? That's what I thought too," she spoke too quickly, her eyes burning with excitement as she sensed in Father Michael a kindred soul.

The next moment her face clouded over.

"Why are they trying to hurt me though and destroy my marriage Father?" I wasn't even born when whatever tragedies happened to them took place. There is such a feeling of evil coming from them yet I have never consciously done anything to hurt anyone." She stopped thinking for a moment, "do people really come back from the dead?"

He paused watching the flames in the fire lick around the logs.

"I realise it is difficult for us having been born into the twentieth century, to understand that such things can happen," he pressed his fingertips together, choosing his words carefully before continuing.

"The desire for life is strong, no let me put it another way, when someone passes over who is unsatisfied with their life, bitter or angry, something appears to happen to their soul. Refusing to accept that the body which housed it is no more, it hovers on the threshold between this world and the next, not wanting to go on and reach the next stage of its journey to everlasting peace. We, in the church, call it 'a soul in jeopardy'. It exists often in cases where there have been traumatic happenings to them in places where they have lived. There is no doubt whatsoever that evil exists in our world, have no doubt of that, however it has been proved that there is something stronger, something which can prevail over evil and that is love."

Jan drew in a small sob, moved by his words.

Father Michael patted her arm, "I'm here to help," he said simply. "However there are things that even I do still not understand."

He stood and walked to the window continuing with his back to her, "It was Edison's theory that if after death our personality survives, then it is perfectly logical and scientific to concede that it retains memory, intellect and all other things learnt whilst alive and that being so, we can conclude that it must be possible for spirits to contact those left behind, or that they feel may be instrumental to them."

"Even those people that were unknown to them in life?"

"Why not? I presume that if one's personalities identify closely with those passed over it could be possible, yes." He paused again, "or it could be that you give off vibrations similar to the spirits own. Unfair as it seems, you could be paying the penalty for something that happened hundreds of years ago."

Jan swallowed as she tried to understand what was being said, her concentration these days was so poor and she had so little understanding of the kind of things Father Michael was talking about.

Father Michael continued, "I do personally believe that our intelligence and personality in the hereafter is capable of affecting matter. Why I believe that Edison even attempted to make a machine with which to measure the effect. It is a well-known fact that after the great Inventors death, three men who had worked closely with him each noted that their clocks stopped simultaneously at 3.24 a.m. the exact time of his death. In Edison's own library the Grandfather clock had also stopped at 3.27 just three minutes after he had passed away. Yes there are indeed more things than we can ever hope to understand."

Jan had to admit, that listening to the gentle Priest speak, everything was beginning to make sense, and found herself wishing that David could have been there to hear what Father Michael had to say.

He sighed, "Evil will always struggle for supremacy over good, we can only pray that eventually the unhappy souls who seem to be lingering on in this house, will be laid to rest and find everlasting peace." He sighed and fingered the heavy silver crucifix he wore around his neck.

"Death is not utter Jan, we do go on and yes, sometimes it appears that we can and do come back, sometimes to comfort, sometimes to make amends and sometimes because something important was left unfinished."

"Does that include returning to wreak revenge also?" Jan asked fearing his answer yet needing to ask the question.

At once it all became too much and without waiting for his reply she covered her face with trembling hands.

"You have been through some dreadful experiences and seen so much, there is a limit to what the human mind can stand". If your theory is correct and there was a woman living here who lost two children, tragic as it is, those souls should now be at peace. However if the deaths were surrounded by evil intent, it could put a different reflection on things.

"You mean an accident?"

"No my dear, I mean....murder."

"Now if you don't mind I would like to say a prayer before I leave."

Jan removed her hands and smiled weakly.

"Please, I'd like that."

Father Michael began to recite the familiar Lords prayer, at once a vigorous pounding sounded above their heads. As Jan saw Father Michael's eyes shoot upwards, she exclaimed with exhilaration.

"You can hear that can't you Father? Please tell me you can hear that."

"I most certainly can."

Jan's relief knew no bounds for at last someone other than she, had heard something not of this world.

Father Michael continued with the prayer, raising his voice ever louder to be heard above the unrelenting pounding from above and now below and all around them.

As the prayer ended so did the pounding.

After the prayer, Jan made a cup of tea for them both, and they chatted as they waited for it to cool.

"Do you think it might be possible for us to find out what really happened here in this house, to be causing such things to take place now? Jan asked hopefully.

"I'm not sure. Maybe. Maybe not. We can certainly begin by piecing together the fragments you have seen, but even then it is like a puzzle, with so many pieces missing, it forms an incomplete picture, " he replied doubtfully. "I have to confess that I know nothing of the history of this house, but the first thing I intend to do is consult the Parish register to see if there have been any accounts of supernatural activity here before. They go back a long way and it could be very interesting to discover what they reveal, although you mustn't get your hopes up, they may reveal nothing at all. It will take a day or so though I'm afraid. Meanwhile you must begin your diary, make sure you note every single incident in as much detail as you possibly can, times and dates included.

Jan nodded, "I will."

"I will get back to you just as soon as possible, I promise. When did you say your husband was due home?"

"In another week."

"I suggest you sleep with both the children in your room until he returns or I get back to you, whichever comes first. The spirits in this house will be angry at my intervention. Things may worsen in the next few days."

"The children have to my knowledge never seen anything Father, nothing at all. Oh Sarah did see the mobile which rotated alone but nothing more."

"Let's hope it continues that way, now if you are at all worried or things do intensify, you must call me. We'll work out a pattern of rings, so you will be able to contact me regardless of static. Let's see, let the phone ring twice then stop then let it ring twice again, do this and I will know you need help and will come immediately."

"Thank you so much Father just hearing you say that makes me feel so much happier."

When he had finished his tea, she saw him to the door and remained watching as he climbed into his little car and with a reassuring nod and wave, drive away.

As she closed the door, Jan felt that an enormous burden had been removed from her shoulders. At last she had been able to talk to someone who had not only listened but also believed her and had actually heard something himself, also he was, thank God, in a position to do something actively to help.

CHAPTER 15

A couple of days later, father Michael arrived in early evening unannounced and somewhat elated. He had been exploring the archived parish records and had found out far more than he had ever expected to about Challoners, he couldn't wait to relay the information to Jan.

Satisfied that the children were sleeping soundly, Jan settled Father Michael in the drawing room and went to make them coffee. When it was ready she carried it in on a tray and set it down on the small table in front of the chesterfield.

Father Michael had taken a slim black, very worn looking book from his suitcase and laying it on his lap, he patted it, saying, "It's all here Jan, everything we needed to know I believe, I will leave it with you to read, but will outline the contents to you briefly. "

He took a sip of coffee before continuing, "The records show that this house has a history of strange happenings and was in fact, the subject of an exorcism, almost thirty years ago. I believe that something has to have opened a doorway to let the spirits back in, something you or David have done perhaps inadvertently."

"Such as?" Jan was curious.

"Hmm I don't know, have you ever used a Ouija board in the house?"

"No, we don't possess such a thing."

"I really don't know what could have been," Father Michael frowned, tapping his chin with his finger.

For some reason, Jan suddenly thought of the old game that Tanza had discovered in the cupboard in the alcove and getting up from her seat, crossed to the cupboard to collect it.

Handing the old chest to Father Michael she said, "We found this, or at least a friend of ours did, the night of our housewarming party, I had thought the cupboard was empty but it wasn't, this was inside. It is a rather strange game, I wonder if that could be anything to do with it?" She paused, "Come to think of it, there was no hint of any strange things happening in the house before that game turned up."

Father Michael opened the chest and removing the contents examined each as he laid them on the coffee table beside the tray. Taking the pack of cards, he turned one over to look at it and his face visibly blanched as he drew in a deep breath, "Oh my goodness," he declared, hastily crossing himself.

"What is it Father? Do you know what the cards say? Are you able to understand Latin?"

"Yes," he murmured quietly, "yes I can understand it," he laid the card down very carefully and subconsciously wiped the hand that had held it, across his gown.

"It is an extremely powerful incantation for use in Black magic ceremonies. I have only ever seen these written in one other place, a book called 'The Grimoire', so dangerous that it is kept under lock and key in the British Museum; only authorised people allowed to view it."

He sighed deeply again, "I don't understand though, unless at least one of these incantations was chanted aloud there would have been no effect."

"They were, Hugh, a friend of ours read a couple out when he was trying to decipher them," explained Jan, "but he had no idea of their meaning."

"I think that could be the answer. That would explain how the spirits were able to return. Now we know what we are up against, I think only another exorcism will rid the house of them again."

He indicated the book he had brought with him; "this book tells that in the 18th century, Challoners was the Manor house and not surprisingly the most important house in the village. Several generations of the same family had lived here and as the years went by, each generation added its own improvements, blocking a window here, adding a tower there and so on. There are a number of building records archived, I didn't bother bringing them along," he took another sip of coffee before continuing.

"There were also a number of photographs, which I have bought along." He delved into his brief case and took out a couple of envelopes, handing the first of them to her.

Jan tipped the half dozen photos out of the envelope on to her lap and sifted through them, all were formal poses, sepia coloured and fading around the edges. As she picked up the last one, she gasped, "I recognise these people," she said breathlessly," at least the woman definitely and the children, I believe they are the children I once saw playing in the wood, I thought I was hallucinating."

She peered at the photo again, "I'm not sure I recognise the man with them although I suppose he could be the man I've seen materialise in this house."

Father Michael then handed her the second envelope.

"See what you make of this one."

Something about the way he said it made her look at him questioningly, then she shook the photo from the envelope.

The portrait, formal again, was of a man probably in his late thirties, standing alone with one hand resting on what looked to be a writing bureau. He wore a high-buttoned shirt beneath a dark suit, the waistcoat of which had a watch chain draped across its front.

"That's him," she whispered, "That's the man who haunts Challoners."

Father Michael nodded with satisfaction.

"I rather thought you were going to say that, Byron Llewellyn, that's his name, an extremely dangerous and evil man in his time, a true abomination in the eyes of the Christian faith.

Something of a gambler, he came from impoverished gentlefolk who lost their money through a series of bad investments. Whilst his parents were solvent, the young Byron enjoyed the high life, spoilt thoroughly for being the only child nothing was denied him. This happy state of affairs continued until he reached his mid twenties when his parents suddenly lost all their wealth.

Byron was bitter; he walked out of the home they had moved to and never communicated with his parents again. His father was heartbroken, the decline in his circumstances coupled with losing his only son, caused him to take his own life, Shocked and entirely unable to cope without servants and her formal social life, Byron's mother went mad and was put into as asylum for the insane, she was to remain there until she died.

Byron showed no remorse or grief when he learned what had happened to his parents. He had begun a totally new life mixing with the lowest of the low in his pursuit of the good life, using people purely for his own ends irrespective of any harm he was inflicting.

He had begun to frequent a club in London's Soho district, a seedy place full of criminals and prostitutes. It was there one evening that he met a man called William Chambers, who by appearances at least, was everything Byron longed to be. Smart successful always with an attractive woman on his arm and on most occasions more than one. Byron was so blinkered by his awe of the man that he never thought to ask himself, why someone so successful and wealthy was regularly to be found in such a place as the seedy nightclub.

Byron took to hanging around William Chambers until at last he was noticed and a conversation began between the two men. Byron found himself relating to the older man all the details of the unfortunate circumstances that he had found himself in and William, a shrewd being, at once noted the greed and hunger in Byron's eyes and knew he had found what he was looking for. William Chambers was a master of the Black Arts and soon Byron became a willing advocate of the unearthly religion against God, feeling that if it had given William wealth and standing in society then doubtless it would do the same for him.

Over the next years he became Williams devoted disciple, drinking, stealing, gambling and womanising became regular pastimes; he regularly found ways of cheating people out of large sums of money for he had a clever master. Only one thing now was missing, a prestigious lifestyle needed a wife that would shine in society. Then one day at the races, he found himself sharing a stand with a well-known magistrate and his daughter Rebecca.

Rebecca caught Byron's eye instantly, for she was indeed a very beautiful girl, in turn Rebecca found herself immensely attracted to Byron.

Byron knew he would have to tread carefully, for it was plain to see that Rebecca was the apple of her father's eye. He began by befriending the man and then asked permission to begin courting his daughter.

The magistrate was at first, extremely pleased that his daughter appeared to have made the acquaintance of a suitable suitor but it was not long before word reached his ears from reliable sources of Byron's depravity and at once the magistrate forbade his daughter to have anything more to do with him.

Rebecca was heartbroken for a while but as time went on, a suitable match was found for her amongst her father's friends and she was married, giving birth over the next four years to two children, a son and then a daughter.

It was a few months following her daughter's birth that things began to happen, terrible things. First the magistrate was killed trampled to death by a runaway horse at a race meeting; this unhappy event resulting in the distraught Rebecca inherited

Challoners, and moved into the house with her family. They had lived there only months when her husband was struck down with a mysterious illness from which he never recovered. Rebecca was beside herself clinging to her children, who were the only family she had left, her mother having died when she was born.

So it was that at a time when she was at her most vulnerable, that Byron Llewellyn put in an appearance again, this time courting the young widow in earnest.

At first Rebecca was hesitant to encourage him out of respect for her dead father. However, she had never been told the reason for her having to cease her relationship with Byron, other than that it had been deemed by her father to be an unsuitable match.

Sensing her obvious reluctance to begin a new relationship with him, Byron turned to his dark magic to assist him in his endeavours, using the help of a willing assistant, a woman who had been involved physically with Byron for a couple of years. So smitten was she with him, that she would do anything for him, even help him gain the favours of another woman, as long as he continued to maintain his relationship with her also. The only attraction this woman held for Byron, was her willing compliance to take part in any of the unnatural sexual practices he insisted upon, and of course that she was also a willing participant in his black magic practices.

Together they carried out a number of unspeakable black masses all with the intent purpose of pursuing the innocent young widow.

Their efforts brought results, for Rebecca unaware that her feelings were being influenced by Black magic, found herself so desperately lonely that she actually welcomed Byron's advances, her mind having been so heavily targeted by the evil pair that she was unable to conceive of any reason why she should turn him away. Within six months he had persuaded her to marry him having made himself so irresistible to her, that she ignored the well- meaning advice of her father's friends when they learnt of the renewal of the unsavoury association.

Having achieved his aim, Byron found that the marriage had not brought him everything he desired, admittedly he now had the wealth and social standing he had craved, but Rebecca although having been married before was still extremely inexperienced in the art of lovemaking, which Byron found extremely unsatisfactory. You must remember Jan, that this was a man used to spending time with and satisfying his lewd desires with prostitutes, skilled in the art of pleasing their clients.

Refusing to allow this one factor to ruin what he had managed to achieve for himself within his marriage, he resolved to bring about a change, once again enlisting the help of his willing and devoted follower, the woman who idolised the ground he stood upon.

Although painfully embarrassed, Rebecca allowed Byron to initiate her into all kinds of sexual acts with which to appease his hunger, for the influence upon her from the spells the two had used, were so great, she was able to deny him nothing. The acts between them became more and more depraved, often even with Byron's devoted woman follower joining in, for by now Rebecca was totally under his spell.

Byron resented the children's presence in the house, wanting his wife entirely to himself. One night, when his lovemaking with his wife was disturbed by one of the children, Byron decided he'd had enough. Within two days both children were dead, seemingly subjects of tragic accidents. Rebecca, seeing clearly for once was heartbroken and committed suicide by throwing herself from a window of Challoners, breaking her neck in the fall. Father Michael paused, "There the story almost comes to a close."

"Jan, realising she had been clenching her hands together the whole time she had been listening to the terrible sad story, relaxed and rested back against the cushions.

"How sad. I wonder who the woman was? The one who helped Byron with his black magic."

"Oh, didn't I say?" Father Michael replied, "All that is known of her is that she was the illegitimate daughter of a street merchant and a prostitute. Her name was Abigail Grinstead."

CHAPTER 15

Jan gasped at Father Michael's words, realising she had not yet told him of her encounter with Abigail, she went on to explain how the woman had arrived one day and then so strangely disappeared.

Thinking things over she then said, "I suppose the sad looking woman must be Rebecca, the coffins I saw, those of her children and the man who materialises, must be Byron Llewellyn, what happened to him after Rebecca killed herself, did he stay on at Challoners? I suppose he would have inherited everything?"

"In the normal way I imagine so, but it seems that the series of deaths were looked upon as highly suspicious and Byron was arrested in a dawn raid upon Challoners, and was found in bed with Abigail. Taken to prison, he was awaiting trial when he mysteriously vanished, in the middle of the night from a locked cell outside of which stood two guards. He was never seen again.

"But how could that be?" Jan was puzzled.

"I imagine he used the dark forces in which he was so skilled."

Jan shuddered.

"There is a little more," Father Michael got up and strode toward the window, looking out at the snow-covered landscape.

"Since that time two families have occupied this house and experienced hauntings similar to those you describe, the first driven out, fleeing in the middle of the night terrified. The second family had the house exorcised, after which it remained free of any haunting until you witnessed it happening all over again."

"I cannot understand father, why no one in the village ever thought to tell David any of these things, he has been to the Pub several times and even in Milborough at the firm where David is employed, there must have been at least someone who had heard something about the house?" Jan was puzzled.

"It's not really so strange, people have a habit of forgetting things they don't want to remember."

Father Michael had left, leaving Jan the book to read for herself.

Paul came downstairs, looking heavy eyed.

"I think an early night would do you some good, young man," she said hugging him. "Let's have an adventure. We'll pretend we are going camping and move your bed and Sarah's cot into mine and daddy's room for a few nights. Would you like that?"

"Okay. I expect you're missing Daddy and want us to keep you company?"

Jan's heart tightened with love for her son.

"Oh I forgot to tell you. Sarah's woken up Mummy."

"All right I'll go and fetch her. Then we'll get some tea."

"Chocolate spread sandwiches?" Paul asked hopefully

"Yes if you like," she ruffled his tawny hair.

After tea the little ones settled in the drawing room watching children's TV. Evening was closing in, Jan felt that of all times of the day, twilight was the worst, hovering between night and day, it was a grey world of sinister shadows, always filling her with the feeling of something unpleasant looming. More and more often she found herself wishing that it were possible for her to open the door and run away, but not only did the agoraphobia prevent it, but the feeling that wherever she went the evil would surely follow, as much a part of her now as was her own shadow. So far she had been able to retain her identity and not be taken over by some of the evil entities, but how long would that state last? Would it end in her losing even her soul? If only it were possible to rid herself of this constant sense of being pursued by some nameless terror, so intense was the feeling that she found it hard to believe, there had ever been a time when she not been mortally afraid.

Jan seized the moment to go to David's study to look for a book she could use as a diary. She was anxious to begin it right away. Not that she would ever forget any of the incidents.

She hurried past the cold spot at the top of the stairs ignoring the voice that began calling her name again and hurried along the landing to the study but stopped with her hand on the doorknob, for beneath the door a light was showing, an eerie, greenish white light.

Without hesitation, preparing herself for the worst, she opened the door flinging it back hard against the wall. So fleetingly it might not even have been there at all, a figure straightened up from the desk. Jan put her hand to her mouth for although it had faded almost immediately it had been seen, it was not before Jan had recognised it as being Abigail Grinstead.

CHAPTER 16

If only David would ring, Jan though worriedly, there had been no call from him for three days and she couldn't understand why.

Although she attempted to reason that he was in all probability snowed under with work, it hurt that he hadn't made time to ring her and make sure that all was well.

She decided she could bear the waiting no longer and went to fetch the piece of paper on which David had written the name of the hotel in Edinburgh, in which he would be staying. She had propped it behind the clock on the mantelpiece in the drawing room.

He'd told her when he left, that she need never ring the hotel, as he would call her each night anyway, but he hadn't done so and she felt more than justified in making the call.

She hoped that the static would not cut in until she had reached him and satisfied herself that there was nothing wrong.

After a few rings, the receptionist at the front desk answered and Jan requested to be put through to her husband's room.

"I'm very sorry madam," came the broad Scottish voice, "but we have no one of that name staying at the hotel."

"But you must have, shall I spell out the name in case you misheard," Jan was confused. She spelt out her surname but the woman insisted there was no one of that name amongst the guests.

Jan put the receiver down slowly, trying to make sense of what she had heard.

Tapping out the number with a trembling hand, Jan's mind was in turmoil, where was her husband, had he got the name of the hotel wrong, it could she realised be something as simple as that. She decided to call Carforth's and speak to David's secretary.

So anxious was she to find her husband's whereabouts, that when the secretary answered the phone, Jan omitted to tell her who was calling. When she asked for David, she was told that he was on a fortnight's holiday and that if she needed to get in touch with him urgently, suggested she ring his home, and without realising who she was talking to the secretary had given Jan, Jan's own number.

Now in a state of shock and becoming very upset Jan thought she must try once again to get in touch with Kate, she had to talk to someone and Kate sprang to mind in the absence of being able to confide in her Mother, who was still at her father's bedside.

She tapped out Kate's number hoping for once that luck would be on her side and Kate would actually be there and answer her 'phone. Knowing of her unsuccessful attempts in the past, Jan decided she would let it ring half a dozen times before giving up.

Just as she was expecting the ansa phone to take over once again, the phone was picked up and a male voice said "Hullo",

Jan dropped the receiver back into the cradle immediately as if it was red hot, for the voice on the other end of the phone had been unmistakably that of her husband, there was absolutely no doubt.

Shaking she sat down at the foot of the stairs, her head in her hands, Kate and David! Why would David be in Kate's flat when he was supposed to be in Scotland and without having told her? There was she realised only one reason, one she didn't want to accept as being true but there was little doubt, David and Kate were having an affair.

Knowing David, he would have instantly rung 1471 to find out who the abruptly cut off call had been from and would know that it had been her. She almost expected him to ring in the next few minutes knowing that she would have put two and two together, after all what other explanation could there be for his not having contacted her, not being where he had said he was, not even telling her he had taken two weeks holiday. It all began to make sense, his irritation with her; over all the things happening in the house, obviously he had turned to Kate whom he felt 'understood him'.

Although over the next days Jan continued to experience psychic attacks, none were as bad as she would have expected them to be, following Father Michaels's visit to the house. Yet, nervously, she felt that the worst was yet to come, and a crescendo was approaching, it was as though the house had drawn in its breath and was holding it, ready to exhale at full blast.

Sarah had begun crawling and was into everything, Jan felt she needed to watch her every moment. There were child locks on all the lower cupboards in the kitchen and Jan felt the time had come to look for and attach the stair gate, to prevent the baby from climbing the stairs. Once she had put Sarah down for her morning nap she began to look for it. She vaguely remembered David storing it in the cellar. Much as she hated to enter the damp, dark rooms below the house again, she knew it was a necessity for Sarah's safety. Luckily she found it relatively quickly as there was little stored in the cellar, the majority of the things they had no use for being stored in the attics.

With difficulty she manoeuvred the heavy box, which contained the gate, up the narrow cellar steps and sitting on the hall floor, unpacked the pieces and proceeded to fix the gate into place. She didn't find it an easy task and found herself cursing David's absence yet again. Finally she felt she had it secured correctly and sat back on her heels quite proud of her achievement. Just then a noise from the top of the stairs distracted her, her heart thudded as she saw an image forming at the top of the stairs. Emerging from a grey dirty mass, a familiar shape was beginning to take form accompanied by a dull roaring sound that hurt her ears. The shape became that of a man, this time he was holding something close to his chest, something that looked like a pillow.

Without looking at Jan the entity began to glide along the landing, some inches from the ground towards the main bedroom where Sarah was taking her nap. Horrified Jan sprang to her feet attempting to wrench the stair gate open. She had secured it too well and precious seconds were lost as she broke her nails and ripped her flesh wrestling to get the catch undone. Having no success, she scrambled over the top and tore up the stairs. As she reached the 'cold spot' she found to her horror that she could precede no further, it was if an invisible wall had dropped in front of her. Frantically, she pushed against it. Feeling it give, she raced into her bedroom, heading straight for Sarah's cot. The room swung crazily as Jan saw the baby laid totally still the upper half of her body obscured by a large white pillow. Hardly daring to look Jan tore the pillow away; she had never known such abject terror as when she saw that her little girl was quite blue and not breathing. Sobbing hysterically she lifted the tiny limp body from the cot and laid her on the bed struggling to force her mind to calm so that she try resuscitation. Why had she never learnt? The answer of course was because she'd never imagined she would need it, no one ever did and to what cost?

Although she feverishly tried everything she knew how, her efforts were fruitless; she was quite unable to revive the baby. Holding her close, she carried her downstairs. She could hear Paul giggling from his place in front of the television set.

Jan stood in the hall clasping the baby's body to her; she didn't know what to do. Tears ran hot and silently down her cheeks as she gasped for breath attempting to slow her frantically beating heart.

How long she stood there she had no idea, when the doorbell rang. Confused at first as to what the sound was she had heard, she at last realised the source and stumbled toward the door and opened it. Father Michael stood there he began to speak, then stopped mid sentence as his gaze fell upon the baby, which wordlessly a pleading look on her face Jan held out to him.

"Ah No, no no," he murmured despairingly and took the little form from her. "Oh my dear whatever has happened?"

Somehow the next few hours passed and Jan was surprised to find that the world around her remained the same in spite of the appalling tragedy that had befallen her. Father Michael did everything for her, sending for the Doctor, the Coroner and the Police all of whom needed to be informed of the baby's sudden death.

Jan behaving in a zombie like fashion expressionlessly replied to questions that were asked of her. Father Michael had explained to her before they had all arrived, that no one would believe her claims that the baby had been suffocated by an entity. Gently he had tried to assure her that it was physically impossible for such a thing to have happened but Jan knew otherwise.

Unable to prevent herself she blurted out the whole story to the Doctor, he listened sympathetically but assured her that the baby's death had been from natural causes and that there was no clinical evidence whatsoever of suffocation. He filled out the Death Certificate and handed it to Jan, her hands shook as she read it, closing her eyes in despair when she reached the cause of death, for the Doctor had written "Classic Cot Death Syndrome".

David was nowhere to be found, in spite of his betrayal, Jan felt she needed him as she never she had before, and she tried calling Kate's flat time and time again, with no result. Finally, the police themselves went to the address Jan had given them and reported back to her that they had no success in finding her husband and that the flat had been vacated, apparently some two days previously.

Standing that evening in the middle of the darkened drawing room, the whispers silent for once, Jan had raised her arms and shouted at the top of her voice, "Satisfied are you now? What else are you going to take away from me?"

She should have known better than to ask.

Jan's only support came from Father Michael. Her Mother was unable to be at the baby's funeral, due to the fact that Jan's father was still clinging to life by a thread and her Mother was afraid to leave his side. Jan, not wishing to add to her Mother's distress managed to assure her that she would cope with Father Michael's help.

Father Michael had contacted a colleague overseas and informed Jan that an exorcism would take place a soon as it could be arranged. The priest authorised to carry out exorcisms was in Venice. It seemed that his services were widely sought, the world over.

When she was told the news that a priest had agreed to carry out the exorcism Jan felt it was too late, she had lost her baby and the evil in the house was now out of control. She dare not let Paul out of her sight for more than a moment, afraid that he too would be taken from her. She longed to flee from the house but two things stopped her, her agoraphobia and the fact that she had no idea where she would go. The funeral had been a double ordeal for Jan, who found she was still suffering the debilitating panic attacks the moment she stepped out of door.

Paul asked for his little sister constantly, he appeared to think that like the cat and his train that had both gone missing, Sarah would simply just turn up again. He spent a great deal of time looking for her which broke Jan's heart for try as she might she could not convince him that Sarah would not be found.

Although a small part of her still mourned the loss of her husband, Jan was extremely bitter towards him and the fact that he could have abandoned them in such a heartless way. She had cried eventually for his loss, then realised that in truth, she had lost him weeks ago, when all the troubles began. She was mourning for what might have been if they had never moved to Challoners.

The only friend in London she had contacted had been Hugh, but he had been away and hadn't returned until after Sarah's funeral was over. She had made no contact with any other of their friends, the only one she would have like to contact being old Abe. She knew however he was too frail to visit and couldn't yet bring herself to break the news to him of Sarah's death.

Father Michael had taken to calling in on her each day, his visits being something for her to depend upon and look forward to. The evil presence in the house creating pandemonium, the moment he stepped through the front door. Although Paul still had seen or heard nothing, Father Michael always wisely chose the evenings to call, when Paul was in bed. Night times were the worse times for Jan, fearful of having happen to Paul the same thing as had her baby, Jan would check on him every few minutes, afraid to put him to bed upstairs without her, she brought him down to sleep on the couch, taking him upstairs only when she herself went to bed. When Father Michael called they would sit in the kitchen, so as not to disturb the little boy.

Finally about ten days after Sarah's funeral Father Michael, breaking his usual habit of calling in the evening, arrived one morning with the welcome news that Father Cristos was travelling to Wales at the weekend and would immediately come to Challoners to carry out the exorcism. For the first time since the baby's death Jan felt her heart lighten at the news. Paul sensed a change in his Mother and was happier than he had been for days.

CHAPTER 17

Father Cristos was feeling tired, agonizingly tired. He stood at the window of his quarters in Venice and looked down over St Mark's square. Pigeons flocked noisily to pick up the crumbs thrown by the few tourists there were around at this time of the year.

The elderly priest had been carrying out exorcisms for the Church over the last twenty-five years. Each had drained his energy anew and tested his faith to the utmost. Now at last, he was beginning to realise it was time he stepped down and let someone younger and stronger take his place. Not just yet however, there was just one more exorcism he was required to carry out before he would retire.

A few days ago he had taken an urgent call from a priest friend in England, Father Michael who had told him of a case needing his expertise. Father Michael had given few details of the troubles surrounding the family in Wales, but what he had detailed had been sufficient for Father Cristos to realise they badly needed his help and without too much delay. He had decided therefore to begin his journey as soon as had been possible. The time had now arrived for him to take the journey to England. The evening before his departure, he spent an hour preparing the things he would need to take with him and put them all in a black leather bag. The last item he carefully wrapped in a scarf, to prevent it from being broken en route. It was a phial of Holy water. All that remained was for him to get a good night's sleep, for he knew he would be called upon to use every ounce of his strength and energy to cleanse the house of the evil that had established itself within the walls of Challoners.

He turned back the smooth starched sheets of the narrow bed in his modest room and climbed in, pulling them up to his chin, how very tired he was, if only he were younger, how much easier it would be, was his last conscious thought before drifting into sleep. Never mind tomorrow I will be on my way towards giving some poor soul some well-earned deliverance.

It was not to be, for sometime during the shadowy hours of early morning, Father Cristos slipped into an even deeper sleep, one from which he would never awaken.

CHAPTER 18

After Father Michael had delivered the news of the exorcism and left, Jan had taken Paul into the kitchen for a glass of milk and some biscuits. Tinsel was scratching at the door in an effort to get out, for the cat flap appeared to have jammed. Jan knelt down upon the floor in an effort to free it, but it was stuck fast, so she went to find something with which to lever it open. Everything that happened next appeared to take place in slow motion. Mewing to get out, Tinsel was becoming agitated, so Paul opened the door to let the little cat out. Although Jan's back was turned for no more than a few seconds, it was long enough for Paul to dart out behind the cat.

"Paul wait," she cried, running toward the door, but he was halfway across the lawn by this time following Tinsel in the snow and laughing.

"Paul come back here this minute," she called angrily, wishing it were that easy, that she could sprint outside after him, but just peering out of the doorway was causing the sweat to break out on her forehead, her legs to turn to jelly and her heart begin hammering.

She expected him to turn round and return at the harsh sound of her voice but he didn't. Instead what she saw turned the blood in her veins to ice water. For Paul continued laughing, then looking up at something she couldn't see, he held out his hand. Gradually a shape took form beside him, the woman and she was leading Paul away in the direction of the wood.

Having to fight her fear of the outdoors Jan took to her feet and fled after them, coatless and only wearing thin slippers she hurtled across the snow, her fear for her son overcoming the terrible symptoms and her awareness of the bitter cold.

Paul in his bright red jersey was getting further and further away, it puzzled her how he could be moving so fast.

Reaching the depth of the woods, Jan kept seeing tantalising glimpses of Paul's scarlet sweater, between the trees and bushes always such a long distance away. The search became a terrible ordeal, fighting off the panic attack in itself enough without the bushes and low branches, which tore at and impeded her progress. Although she called Paul constantly and listened for a reply, none came, the only sound being that of the wind moaning eerily between the branches of the dark trees. Panting she lurched on, uncaring of the bitter cold, knowing only that somewhere in this infernal wood, her son was being led away from her toward what? She fell awkwardly catching her foot on a tree root concealed by snow. She fell heavily, face first, twisting her ankle on the rough ground, sending a bolt of pain shooting up her leg. Gasping, she scrambled to her feet brushing the stinging snow crystals from her face. She took the next step tentatively finding it quite agonising, but carried on, half running and half limping fearful of losing sight of her son, her only aim to catch up with him.

The wind rose to a crescendo, whipping her hair across her smarting eyes, snow whipped up from the ground to meet the swirling flakes falling from above. Her progress made even more difficult by the strength of the wind, Jan pressed on determinedly.

She hadn't realised she was nearing the lake until the trees began to thin out. Horrified she realised then that she had lost sight of Paul. Allowing a moment to stop for breath she held on to a tree for support as she raised her injured foot from the ground, swelling fast it throbbed mercilessly and she knew that the last thing she should be doing was put weight upon it. Trying desperately to ignore the painful throbbing, he gaze scanned the wood from side to side but there was no sign of Paul in any direction.

"Paul, Paul," she cried, "Mummy's coming, where are you? Call out to me so I can find you." but there was no reply, no sound at all in fact other than an occasional soft slithering sound as snow slid from over laden branches to the ground.

Bitterly cold, her teeth clenched and trying to push from her mind, the agonizing pain in her ankle and her overwhelming fear of the outside, Jan pressed on along the shore of the lake. Scanning the waters edge for some sign of her son she saw nothing of him or the entity that had enticed him away from the house. Desperately frightened she continued around the lake, now too full of fear to even care about the bitter cold or the fierce pain in her ankle. Her throat was becoming sore from her constant calling out for her son.

At last her heart leapt for on the far shore she caught a fleeting glimpse of bright red. Hobbling as fast as she could she made her way toward it. At last she was able to see in detail what she had glimpsed. Only one other moment in her entire life matched what she felt as she gazed at Paul face down in the freezing water close to the shore. Without hesitation, her heartbeat pounding her ears, she stepped into the freezing water and fought to free his body from the weeds and rushes entangled around his legs. Raising him in her arms, freed at last she stood knee deep in the frozen water looking into the sky and howled, in the primeval wail reminiscent of the howls of grief heard the world over in the face of such dreadful accidents. Of the entity there was no sign.

Stumbling to the bank she attempted resuscitation, knowing in her heart that it was futile, yet she had to try. At last she lay down beside Paul pulling him close as if to warm him and take away the terrible white pinched look on his little face. She held his wet icy cheek against her own and closed her eyes.

Finally drifting into unconsciousness, from shock cold and exposure, she lay beneath the winter sky that opened, releasing soft white flakes of snow that drifted down covering the two figures in a blanket that gave no warmth.

Father Michael was suffering from a bad head cold. With eyes streaming and constant sneezing, he found driving difficult as he approached Challoners that afternoon. He knew he should probably have waited until he felt better but he was anxious to make sure that Jan and Paul were alright, having woken with a terrible premonition that all was not as it should be. He would be as utterly relieved as Jan when the exorcism finally took place.

Cautiously negotiating the icy snow banked by the wind, in frozen ridges in the drive entrance, he steered through the gateway, wondering again when the hard winter would lose its grip. Fresh snow had again cloaked the countryside in sparkling white overnight.

Bringing the car to a halt before the steps to the front door, Father Michael's heart fluttered in alarm as he saw the door standing wide open. His premonition appeared to have been correct; something had to be terribly wrong.

Leaping from the car as fast as his cumbersome gown would allow, he left the car door open and took the steps to the house two at time, almost slipping and losing his balance in his fevered anxiety to get inside. In the hall he stood for a moment and listened, the house was quiet, too quiet. A quick search revealed that no one was there, where could they be?

The thunderous pounding on the ceiling, which had almost always greeted Father Michael's visits then broke the silence, in agitation he ignored it.

The thick snow which still fell had wiped out any slight chance of finding footprints to follow. Father Michael knew that because of Jan's agoraphobia, something major would have caused her to lead the house, however afraid she was to remain there. Again it was impressed upon him, what a dilemma she lived in afraid to leave yet afraid to stay.

He struggled to regain rational thought and glanced briefly at the telephone on the hall table, but past experience had proved that the evil seeping through this house would not allow any call for help to be made. However common sense told him he must at least make the effort, whatever the outcome. Lifting the receiver he dialled 999, he had not even heard the first ring before the thunderous pounding increased and electrifying static ended the call he was trying to make.

Wasting no more time, Father Michael left the house and drove towards the village at death defying speed in the harsh weather conditions. Nearing the village, he slowed aware that he was approaching a curve in the road. As the curve came into sight, a dark mass took shape in the road just ahead and rolling towards him, enveloped the car in a thick dark fog. Unable to see where he was going the priest attempted to bring the car to a halt. At the speed he was travelling hitting the brake did only one thing, send him into a skid on black ice concealed beneath the snow, resulting in the car plunged down the steep slope at the side of the road, landing upside down in a field.

It was two hours before a passing motorist, glancing out of the side window, saw the dark object in the snow covered field and realised that it was an upside down car. With heart pounding he brought the car to a halt and leapt out scrambling down the bank. He wondered how long it had been since the accident had happened and if anyone was inside still, needing help.

Dropping to his knees in the thick snow, he peered through the window, the ice had formed thickly on the glass and due to that and the dim light of late afternoon, he was unable to see anything. He scraped the ice from the glass and looked again, this time making out a man who was still strapped into his seat upside down, apparently either unconscious or worst still possibly dead. He immediately retuned to his car, driving as quickly as the road conditions allowed to the village to alert the Police and the Ambulance.

As luck had it and maybe God was looking out for his own, the paramedics found upon their arrival that miraculously Father Michael was still alive and without any life threatening injuries. Unconscious however, he was freed from his car and carried to the ambulance, where he came round en route to the hospital in Milborough. At once he became extremely agitated as his memory came back to him and he saw again what had taken place before the car had left the road.

Although the paramedics attempted to calm him, he insisted they hear what he had to say. He became even more agitated when he realised how long he had been trapped in the car for he knew that precious time had been lost in finding the whereabouts of Jan and her little boy. As soon as he had finished explaining the reason for his extreme anxiety, the paramedics radioed the Police who immediately despatched a unit with tracker dogs to Challoners, to search for the missing woman and her son.

Meanwhile tied to his hospital bed by sheer necessity Father Michael lay frustrated, wishing he could be a part of the search team. It was now in the hands of others he could do nothing but wait, which was the hardest part of all. He closed his eyes sending up an earnest prayer that the news when it came would be good.

A thorough search of the house, attics and cellar had revealed no sign of the missing woman and her small son, so the search was turned to the grounds surrounding Challoners.

Systematically the police and dogs tracked the woods inch by inch until a dog's frantic barking signalled to the others that something had been found.

At first glance, the worst was feared, Jan was however still alive, although barely, her breathing shallow, and her pulse weak. Ironically the thick snow she hated so much had helped to keep her alive. They had to prize Paul's body from her frozen arms, so tightly was he held against her. There was not a single member of the search team who had not been deeply saddened and extremely moved by the discovery, for as in every one of their searches they always hoped to find everyone alive.

In the days that followed Jan hovered in a twilight world between life and death. Once conscious she slept for long periods, hoping each time she slept that she wouldn't wake again, having lost everything that made her life worth living. Each time she woke her sobs of anguish for her children tore the very hearts of those who cared for her. They knew she had lost the will to live, wanting only to be with her children wherever that may have been.

A few days later she was well enough to be taken to a telephone and speak to her Mother who was still keeping her anxious vigil at her husband's bedside. From David and Kate, there was still no communication whatsoever. If David had learnt of any of the tragic events, he had not made contact.

The days passed in painful agony of a loneliness and grief, she could never have imagined. Then one afternoon, whilst sitting on the enclosed hospital balcony, she had a surprise visitor, it was Hugh.

Although he tried tactfully to ask a few questions of her, Jan was reluctant to talk about the house, or the evil she knew had brought about the tragic events. She found it far too painful still to mention the children she'd loved so, neither had she any inclination whatsoever to discuss David or Kate. Hugh found it difficult in fact to have any kind of conversation with her, for there were so many subjects, which were taboo. She was locked in her painful world and resented anyone attempting to enter, even in an attempt to console her. All she would talk about was the hospital staff and other patients and Hugh could see quite clearly that even that was an effort she would rather not have to make.

Before he left her, he suggested that she come and stay with him in London when she was discharged from Hospital. To his alarm Jan burst into tears at this suggestion, explaining that it was purely from relief as she had been worrying where she could go when she left hospital, a worry she had not voiced yet to the people taking care of her. Were it not for her father's illness she would have gone home to her Mother.

Of course she knew she would have to return to Challoners at least once, if only to collect the things she needed or wanted to keep, but she had no wish to stay there longer than was absolutely necessary.

She had learned that the exorcism had not been carried out. Father Michael when well enough had begged to be allowed to visit her and was taken by wheelchair to her ward from his own. He had explained sorrowfully that whilst in the hospital himself he had been visited by a Church elder who had informed him of Father Cristos' death. No suitable replacement for the Exorcist had yet been found, although he understood, it was a matter of urgency that someone be found as quickly as possible.

Try as she might, Jan couldn't help herself from feeling that it was all part of a master plan, the children, Father Michaels's accident, Father Cristos' illness, even her own stay in the hospital. How widely spread this evil emanating from Challoners had become. Not only had she lost her beloved children and her husband but also felt indirectly responsible for Father Michael's accident and the death of a priest she had never even met.

At last, the day arrived when she was to be released from hospital, the staff that had taken care of her giving her a good send off when Hugh arrived to collect her. Jan had felt safe in the hospital, as safe as she was able to feel anywhere and she felt the familiar panic forcing its way up from her chest as they approached the hospital exit. Hugh, supporting her, gave her arm a comforting squeeze and she found the ordeal of crossing the car park to where Hugh's car stood waiting, slightly less of a problem than she had imagined it would be.

Neither of them spoke much the few miles to Challoners, it was still bitterly cold and there were remnants of snow still clinging to the verges of the road they travelled. The plan was that Hugh would drop her at the house to pack up a few things she needed, whilst he drove to the village to arrange for someone to come and close up the house and take away the things she no longer wanted to keep.

Hugh wasn't happy about her going into the house alone, but Jan was insisting upon it, although she didn't know why, she felt strongly that it was something she needed to do.

During the journey, Jan's heart was thudding in anticipation of how she would feel back inside the house which had destroyed her life. The anticipation growing stronger as the car turned into the driveway. Her palms grew damp and a wave of nausea swept over her as the house came into view, looking to her every bit as forbidding as it had ever done.

Hugh brought the car to a stop in front of the steps. Climbing out he opened her door and helped her to her feet; she was very weak and somewhat unsteady.

"Let me at least help you to the door," he pleaded.

Jan shook her head, "No, you get off to the village Hugh, I won't be long, I don't want to stay here any longer than I have to, don't worry I'll be fine."

Hugh reluctantly got back into the car and watched her thin pale-faced figure slowly climb the wide steps and enter the front door.

Just before she closed it she looked up and gave him a slow smile, then the closing door hid her from view. Shaking his head half afraid to leave but knowing it was what she wanted, he started the engine and drove away.

After she closed the door Jan found herself trembling uncontrollably, no one would ever know what it had cost her to enter this house again. Her legs felt like jelly almost too weak to hold up her painfully thin frame, she had lost so much weight over the last few months. Her breathing was fast and shallow, her heart was leaping in her chest at frightening speed, for she was mortally afraid. She stood as if rooted in the hall, listening but the house was intensely and alarmingly quiet, she wasn't sure quite how she had expected it to be, but if the presence had been waiting for her return surely something would happen soon.

Forcing her feet to move one before the other, unsteadily she walked slowly from room to room beginning with the kitchen. Everything appeared to be wrong, it was too normal except for the row of potted violets on the windowsill which were quite dead. Tinsels food dishes still sat on the floor, they had been emptied and cleaned, and Hugh had told her that the little cat was being looked after by one of the villagers until such time as she wanted her back. With a last glance around the room, she left it closing the door quietly behind her.

The next room she looked inside was the old library, nothing had ever been done with it, it stood silent empty still.

Making her way into the Drawing room she was shocked to see Paul's train left lying on the floor where he had played with it last. Seeing it brought a painful lump to rise in her throat and she was unable to prevent the deep sob, which escaped her lips. She forced herself to pick up the train for this was something she wanted to take with her.

On and on through the house she made her last sad pilgrimage, gathering in a small pile on her bed the pitifully few items she wanted to take away with her. Hugh had already collected her clothes a few days previously and taken them to his flat, all that remained was for her to gather together personal items.

Opening the closet, she found a small hold all and stuffed everything inside, Paul's, train, Sarah's teddy, her grandmothers musical box, one or two sentimental knick knacks her parents had given her over the years and a few small pieces of semi precious jewellery she owned, which one day would have been Sarah's. As she wrapped these last few items in an old silk scarf her gaze was caught by a glint from her wedding ring, which she still wore on her finger. It was too big now and twisting it around, a fresh wave of nausea swept over her as it reminded her anew of David betrayal and desertion. She crossed to the window, throwing it wide open, then slipped off the ring and without a second thought tossed it out into the snow. Closing the window, she zipped up the bag and left the room.

As she walked down the stairs she realised with a start that the 'cold spot' was no longer there. The house had remained quiet the whole time she had been in it, completely normal, she couldn't understand why, unless of course the spirits having achieved their aim had now gone to rest. With this thought coursing through her mind, she sat on the stairs in the hall and awaited Hugh's return.

Time ticked on, 'surely he'll be back soon,' she though, wearily closing her eyes.

"Jan, Jan, Jan," the voice broke the silence, her eyes flew open and she looked around terrified.

When oh when would it stop and leave her in peace? The voice persisted along with the awareness of something not altogether unfamiliar. Something, some forgotten memory was stirring in the back of Jan's mind, she groped to reach it but it had slipped beyond her grasp.

At once, her feelings of anxiety and fright were replaced by the strangest feeling, which suffused her being like a warm nebulous mantle. An overwhelming serene calm encircled her, such as she had not experienced for the longest time. Opening her eyes, relishing the warm safe feeling, she found to her amazement that she was lying in a bed. Warm sunlight was streaming through the window laying golden rays across the sheet which covered her prone body.

CHAPTER 19

"Jan, Jan, can you hear me?" the voice said again followed by "Nurse, nurse come quickly, I think she is waking up. Jan, Jan darling can you hear me?"

Slowly, for she found her neck was very stiff, she turned her head in the direction of the voice. David sat by the bed and was, she realised, holding tightly on to her hand. He wore a frown yet hope and anticipation shone from his sky blue eyes.

"Jan oh Jan darling you've come back to us." Tears were rolling down his cheeks unchecked, it was, Jan realised, the first time she had ever seen her husband cry.

She closed her eyes again experimentally, what was this, how did she come to be in this bed in what was obviously a hospital room? When she opened her eyes again, would it all still be here?

She did so and everything was still the same. Flowers filled the room, Roses, Carnations, lilies, all her favourites, now she was able to smell the heady fragrance they gave off in the small enclosed space, laced with another odour, that of hospital antiseptic.

"What am I doing here?" she asked, her voice cracked, her throat hurt and her mouth was painfully dry. For in her mind just seconds ago she had been sitting on the stairs in Challoners waiting for Hugh to collect her.

A nurse stepped quickly forward and gently raising her head offered her a drink of water.

Jan pushed her away suddenly remembering something important she had to know, "David where are the children?" She became extremely agitated.

David smoothed her brow,

"Sssh," he whispered, "they are absolutely fine, with your Mother, longing to see you as soon as you are a little better. Don't try to talk too much, you've been asleep a very long time, your vocal chords are out of practice."

"What do you mean, how long?" she looked pleadingly into David's face pleading for the answer.

"Four months to be exact darling, don't you remember anything from before, anything at all?"

Jan struggled to remember. All she could think about was the fact that her mind was chock full of terrible memories of strange and frightening things that had happened to her in Challoners, it seemed impossible to imagine they had been products of her own mind.

Sensing her need to have some sort of explanation before she would quieten, David began to fill in just a few of the details.

"You fell, badly. Do you remember moving into the new house at all?"

Jan nodded.

"You insisted on climbing steps to hang curtains in the drawing room, but the legs of the steps were unevenly placed and they toppled over, you fell hitting your head on the fireplace. You went from unconsciousness into a very deep coma," he breathed back a sob, "I, we, thought you were going to die."

Jan took the offered drink from the nurse before speaking again.

"I don't remember any of that just living at the house and such terrible things happening. David the house was haunted," she began to grow agitated again David squeezed her hand.

A Doctor had just entered the room and overheard her last words. He perched himself gently on the opposite side of the bed to David and took her wrist checking her pulse rate, and then he smiled at her encouragingly.

"We are still very much in the dark where coma patients are concerned, from all appearances your mind was completely closed down, due to the very deep state of unconsciousness caused by severe inflammation of the brain. However it is possible that you may have been accessing memories at such a deep level, that we were unable to measure the brains activity. There have been processes going in your brain that frankly we don't understand and hallucinations are all part of it I am sure.

"So why have I woken now?"

"I think the presence of someone who loves you close by the bedside at all times has helped. David was here every day or at least part of it and constantly called you back."

So that had been the voice constantly calling her name, Jan realised in wonder, no wonder it had sounded strangely familiar.

As the weeks turned into months," the Doctor continued, "we tried to persuade David to spend less time here, as there was no response from you. After all as I am sure you realise life has to go on and he'd spent so much of his time here over the last weeks. We tried telling him that he could still be sitting here waiting for you to wake up in a year, two years time and you would still be comatose.

He refused to give up and thankfully it would seem that he was right, he winked at David, and we were wrong and I am very glad that we were. He patted her hand and stood up.

"Now its time you rested and slept, no don't worry," he quickly reassured her seeing blatant panic in her eyes." It will be real sleep and this time you will wake up."

"I won't be far away darling I promise," David, said, "by the time you wake I'll be back again."

"Will you bring the children? Oh please David," seeing a look of doubt pass between him and the Doctor. "I need to hold them again so very much, ", she pleaded.

The Doctor nodded imperceptibly.

"All right but just for a few minutes."

Jan sunk back into the pillows as David followed the Doctor out of the door. The Nurse settled the pillows comfortably around her head and asked if she was comfortable, Jan nodded that she was fine.

For a little while she pondered over all she had been told, why she wondered if it had all been illusion brought about by her damaged swollen brain, had it all seemed so real, they had been memories of real occurrences to her. She was still trying to make sense of it when she drifted into sleep.

The next few days Jan went from strength to strength.

David had bought the children in several times along with her parents who were staying at Challoners with David until she came home. Her joy had known no bounds at holding her children and feeling them alive and warm. To see her dad, healthy as he had always been, not having suffered the heart attack her brain had conjured up whilst comatose, a further joy.

Kate had been to visit as well, bearing a gorgeous bouquet of early summer flowers. Burying her nose in the delicate fragrance, brought it back to Jan that she had missed four months of her life for it was May now.

As Kate hugged her, her familiar perfume brought tears to Jan's eyes. Kate told her how she had visited often; giving David a needed break and had spoken to her constantly in the hope that something she said would help bring Jan back.

At long last, Jan was told she was well enough to go home.

Home, she still though of the flat as home, after all apparently she had only been in the house one day when the accident had taken place.

When she was collected from the hospital by David and driven home, Jan expected to see a snow covered world outside, but of course it wasn't. The trees were vibrant, green with new life and the fields on the way to Challoners were full of grazing lambs. A few late primroses studded the banks of the lane's verges and bluebells nodded their heavy heads in the slight breeze.

David turned the car into their drive, Jan felt familiar nervousness washing over her, everything she had imagined had happened being still too fresh in her mind, then the house came into view and Jan gasped for it looked stunningly inviting and vastly different.

Whilst she had been in hospital David had hired a team of builders and decorators to transform the old house. Painted a soft pale cream, it had undergone a dramatic transformation such as she could have not have believed possible. The diamond panes of the many windows twinkled in the warm sunlight, flowers bloomed in the borders, tidy and weed free, the magnificent front door was grey no longer but a bright sunny yellow and had a shining brass letterbox and knocker, the rusty old lantern above the porch had gone.

The lawn beyond the house was neatly mown in stripes and the rhododendron bushes a blaze of pink, purple and scarlet blooms. Birds sang and the sky was a cloudless blue, she could hardly believe the transformation.

As they drew up before the door it flew open and Paul came running down the steps calling "mummy, mummy you're home," behind him tottered Sarah.

"She's walking," Sarah marvelled as the baby climbed carefully down the steps towards her Mother and grabbed her around her knees.

Over the next few weeks Jan couldn't believe she could have been so ecstatically happy, her life had been given back to her. So what if now and again she heard a faint whisper or had the feeling someone was behind her, she knew now it was nothing but imagination. Traces of left over memories in her almost fully recovered mind.

After a prolonged leave of absence, kindly given him by his employers, David finally returned to work. Jan was on her own once again, her parents having left a week after her return from hospital anxious to get back to their own home again, now they were assured their daughter was safe and well.

One lovely warm summer day, Paul and Sarah were playing happily on the lawn with a ball. Jan hummed as she polished furniture pausing every now and again to check on the children; still somewhat reluctant to let them out of her sight she was gradually feeling less anxious.

Hearing the doorbell ring, she put down the cloth and polish and hurried across the hall to open the door, smoothing her hair back away from her face. She could still not get used to its being short, but it had needed to be cut due to her head injury.

She opened the door; the bright sun behind the figure at the door at first making it difficult for Jan to make out who was there.

As the figure gradually became clear, loud booming sounds filled Jan's head, her mouth dried and her whole world shifted subtly sideways.

The woman on the doorstep didn't smile. Her grim face looked disdainfully at Jan as she said.

"Good morning I'm Abigail Grinstead."

THE END

Printed in the United Kingdom
by Lightning Source UK Ltd.
102302UKS00001B/34